Olivia Truluck
A woman who persevered and never gave up.

CONTENTS

CHAPTER ONE
MISSOURI

On April 27, 1899, the day I turned 10 years old, Mama Rose gave her rambunctious daughter, ten swats on the rear end with a hickory stick, plus one more for good measure. As Daddy helped himself to a piece of my birthday cake, he remarked that young Negro girls like me, who were especially lively, scared the bejesus out of those whose skin was lily white. At the time, I gave scant thought to what some called the great amalgamation or the mixing of Negros and whites. As far as my decade old brain was concerned, white folks were to be avoided like the plague, especially those who paraded around wearing bed sheets and burned crosses. Right here and now, I'll acknowledge the corn and confess that I was a bundle of energy who had a mind-set on one day leaving the low wattage farm for the high voltage cities of K. C. or St. Louie.

Our homeplace was situated in the southwestern corner of the 'Show Me' state. Up to that time I'd spent my entire life with my feet mired in rich black sandy loam. Our two-room home was close to the Tebo Creek, the meandering stream that bordered the entire eastern boundary of Daddy's 41 acres.

Daddy called our farm, "An earthly paradise."

And it was, at least for a while. Ever the practical one, my Mama always said, "Ain't nothin' gonna' last forever."

It was the day after my tenth birthday that a traveling gypsy-lady

1

paid a visit to our farm. Life in 'Dullsville' immediately brightened, but my happy expression quickly drooped when Mama told the aged woman, "Thank you, Ma'am, but with us bein' Christian members of the Church of the First Born, we don't abide by no palm readin' or crystal ball gazin'."

My ears perked and a smile grew when I heard Daddy say, "That's nonsense, Rose. Let the woman lay down her cards. What can it hurt?"

The old Creole woman wore a faded blue turban that hid all her hair, that is if she had any to hide. She was draped in colorful silk dress dotted with bangles and beads.

Daddy whispered, "The fortune teller looks like a one-woman medicine show where the cocaine cure is worse than the disease."

At first, I was taken aback when she placed the deck of Tarot cards on our kitchen table, right where my birthday cake had set the day before, but then realized it was either there or the floor. Ever so slowly, one at a time, the seer turned the cards face up. She studied the wild array of colorful figures and symbols printed on each card, until finally, she pointed with her bony forefinger. Mama, Daddy, and me on tiptoes, leaned over the table to eyeball the drawing of an ancient one who was pointing up in the air with one hand and down to Hades with the other. The robed man or woman, I couldn't be sure, was standing next to a table. Above the person's head floated a squiggly figure 8 lying on its side. The reader will be glad to know that I've since come to learn the impossibility of infinity.

"Ahhhh...the Magician," the crone whispered. "As above, so below."

"Hmmmmf," Mama huffed. "Above is God, below is the Devil."

"And in between up there and down here are the Trulucks," the gypsy cackled, pointing her sharp fingernail directly at me. "But don't despair. The Magician gives the power to overcome all obstacles."

Daddy chuckled. "The only obstacle I have a farmin' on the Tebo is the gol' dang flint rock hidin' in the ground."

"Ahhhh...but there will come other impediments."

As the crone gathered her cards into a neat stack, I blurted, "Like what?"

When the old gypsy lady turned her furrowed forehead toward

me, I could see a thousand years of wisdom in her watery blue-gray eyes. "Not to worry, child. The Trulucks will persevere."

"Well," Mama said, laughing somewhat nervously. "That's some right good news, I'd say."

"Sure is," Daddy said, and confirmed Mama's announcement by slapping his knee. "On that note, why don't we have some refreshments?"

When a quart jar of moonshine magically appeared, the old crone nodded and cackled, "Don't mind if I do, but only for my lumbago."

****

Ten-year-old kids don't look beyond 'what's for dinner', much less a gypsy lady's prognostications. Children of that particular age, if they're normal, are like a flock of turkeys, that live in the moment.

By the next day, I had forgotten all about Tarot cards and obstructions. After Mama's delicious supper of buttered cornpone and collard greens boiled with ham hocks, Daddy leaned back in his chair with a pop of his suspenders. It was candle lighting time and the magic hour when he always fired up his favorite corncob pipe. Daddy huffed and puffed a few times, sending up smoke signals which was a sign for me and my kid brother, Jerome, to gather 'round for one of Daddy's long, tall-tales.

When he spoke, the sound of his hoarse voice was low and rumbly. "Mmmmm, let me see…it was sometime after the war that we came to be here…back in seventy-nine, if I'm not mistaken. That right, Mama?"

"No, Dear. It was in Seventy-six, the same year a locomotive crossed the Great Divide."

"By gosh, you're right, Mama," Daddy exclaimed. "Jumpin' Jehoshaphat, woman. You got the elephant's memory."

"And eagle eyes," I added.

Daddy continued. "Eighteen-seventy-six it was – by jiminy. That was the year we left Mississippi and ended up in Missouri."

"Why, Daddy?" Jerome asked, in his irritating nasal tone of voice. "Why did you and Mama leave Mississippi?"

"Because," Daddy grumbled. "After the war we Negros were catawamptiously chewed up and beat down."

"What your daddy's saying, sweet darling," Mama Rose countered while placing the can of tobacco back up on the fireplace mantle, "Dame Fate is the course for the man who fails to act."

"Meanin', Stringbean," Daddy said, calling me by my nickname. "If we hadn't skedaddled from the Southland, we'd still be nothin' but poor sharecroppers, slavin' for the man. But here in Missouri, we own the land we live on, free and clear. It's all ours…and there ain't nothin' more important than that."

"Your story, that's important too, right Daddy?" Jerome asked. Right here I'd like to confess that Jerome's whiny voice sometimes drove me up the wall. With all his other bad, nasty habits, my brother's only saving grace was that he played the flute like an angel.

Daddy laughed when he patted the top of Jerome's nappy head and nodded. "Yes, it is, my boy. Yes, it is. Now, where was I?" Daddy situated his rear end deeper into the woven-cane, oval-back rocking chair and puffed a couple of more times on his pipe. Once his dark brown face reappeared from out of the cloud of white smoke, he looked at me, then Jerome. "If I remember correctly those Washingtonian carpetbaggers turned out to be right friendly people. When I showed up at their office, it was like I was the first Negro they'd ever laid eyes on. By jingles, I got my back patted and my right hand pumped up and down so many times I thought my arm was about to fall, clean off. Let me tell you, young'uns, not only did I get my old boots shined, one of those nice guv'ment men gave me a chit for a free shave and a haircut down at the Negro saloon. Man, I thought I'd died and gone to hog heaven."

"You did, Dear," Mama Rose said, while bending over and using the corner of her apron to wipe dewberry jam from Jerome's chubby cheeks. "And as far as carpetbaggers are concerned, I would think it's easy to be generous with other people's money."

"Like I was sayin'," Daddy grumbled, "if Uncle Sam was givin' away forty acres and a mule to any person of color willing to hitch himself to the task, who was I to argue?"

"Hold your horses, Daddy" I interjected. "I thought we have forty-one acres."

"I thought so, too," Jerome the copycat, whined.

"You're right a rain. It says right on the deed of trust. Forty-one acres." Daddy got a serious look on his face, then he pointed to a tintype sitting on Mama's little oval tea table. "Right there. That's my ol' Pappy Truluck. That'd be your Gran-pappy Truluck. He's the one who was responsible for getting' us God's extra acre." Daddy's grumbly voice got real low. "It was back during the great conflict between the states. Pappy Truluck ran from his master in Mississippi. He high tailed it all the way to Kansas. That's how he came to be a private first-class, in the 1st Kansas Colored Volunteer Infantry. That extra acre was a "thank you" from Uncle Sam for Pappy's loyal service to the Union Army of Emancipation."

Long after Daddy finished his story, I sat alone on the front porch thinking about my liberation from the farm. Although, I loved our 41 acres, I yearned for a city that might offer more intellectual stimulation than Ned's Third Grade Reader. I wanted to see the world, not just read about it. The only sources of excitement that occasioned to stop in our neck of the woods were the passing tinkers, gypsies and hawkers.

I looked up into the night sky and whispered, "Star light, star bright, my wish for tonight, show me the way to Bountiful."

****

Since the Tebo Creek bordered our 41 acres, Daddy only had to dig a hole ten or twelve feet deep before finding water. The well was located up close to the house so Mama wouldn't have to walk too far with a heavy bucket. It seemed like every time I saw Mama, she always was carrying something. Daddy said that Mama Rose was born with a green thumb on one hand and a broom in the other. When she planted a lilac bush next to the newly dug well before I even got here, I heard-tell that Daddy laughed his fool head off. Miss Linnie, Daddy's spinster auntie, said that Mama stuck that scrawny twig in the ground and told it to grow.

It was one evening after supper, when we were all sitting at the dinner table listening to Jerome play The Sidewalks of New York, on his flute, that I looked out the window. Respectful of an artist's time in the spotlight, I waited until the music stopped before speaking.

"Mama, exactly what time of the year did you plant the lilac bush?"

"Well, my Dear, I believe it was around mid-April."

"You sure, Mama?" Jerome asked, placing his bamboo flute on the table. "That was a long time ago. Before I was born even, wasn't it?"

"Yes, Dear, it was. I remember the dogwood trees." Mama had

5

her eyes closed and a smile on her lips. "The branches were hanging heavy, covered with so many pretty white flowers, it looked like it had just snowed."

"Now that you mention it, that's not exactly how I remember it at all," Daddy said, while using an ivory-colored penis bone taken from a racoon, to pick strands of venison from the gap between his two front teeth. "It was hot that day, hotter than blue blazes and the cow lilies were in bloom."

"So, it must've been in July, right Daddy?" I questioned.

Suddenly, at the other end of the table from where I sat, Miss Linnie, raised her head up from buttering another chunk of cornpone. In a voice just loud enough to be heard, she said, "Chil', don't listen to a word of what that man says. Why, he can't even recollect from yesterday, where he laid his pipe down today."

****

Later that same evening, after finishing with the dishes, Mama and I were still in the kitchen. I hung my wet dishrag on the drying rack and pointed out the window.

"Mama, why do we still call that a lilac bush?"

"What do you mean, Dear?"

"How tall is a bush?"

Mama shook her head and held her hand about shoulder high.

"Have you seen the lilac bush lately, Mama?"

"Of course. I look at it every day on my way to the well."

"And how tall would you say that bush is?"

"Mmmmm," Mama hummed. "About as tall as the outhouse."

"Well, do you remember telling me to only believe a third of what I see, a fourth of what I think I know, and nothing of what I hear?"

"Yes, Dear, I remember telling you that."

"So, if a third of seeing is true, then why isn't that lilac bush called a tree?"

****

From that day forward we called Mama's lilac bush a tree, but to me it was my home away. I had to crawl on hands and knees through a hole in the low hanging branches to get inside where I'd sit next to the main tree-trunk and take inventory of the items in my secret nest. Along with my collection of odd rocks, clam shells, lucky buckeyes and arrowheads that I'd found down by the Tebo, there also was a small chalkboard and chalk.

Living in the boondocks such as we did, most of my friends were made up. Of course, I'd never met anyone who came close to being well-known or famous; that is unless we count Mister Washington, the old man who lived two farms over from our place. Mister Washington claimed to have shaken hands with the Great Emancipator, himself. Although, according to Daddy, Mister Washington didn't actually meet Abraham Lincoln while he was still walking upright. It was at the state funeral, where our neighbor touched the cold hand of the dead president.

All throughout the summer of '99, listening to the sound of tiny grey birds with sharp beaks, chirping like they owned the lilac tree, I spent hours under the spreading branches. I loved to watch the whorls of green leaves flutter in the wind, along with the lavender flower clusters that hung down like giant grapes. They looked good enough to eat, but I knew from past experience they tasted like dead wormwood. The sweet fragrance sometimes left me lightheaded. One day I asked Mama if a person could get tipsy sniffing lilac blossoms. She shook her head and said, "No, Dear, if you do get dizzy or see strange things, it's only your imagination playing tricks on you."

An early cold-snap came in mid-September. The bountiful lilac blooms shriveled, the wind blew, and they were no more. But my nest was still protected with an abundance of leaves that hadn't fallen. It was a good thing, too, because that foliage is why I'm still alive to tell my story.

CHAPTER TWO
MISERY

Exactly which tree or flower was in bloom when the lilac twig was put in the ground was not the only incident that Mama Rose and Daddy disagreed on. For instance, they both had different opinions as to when Indian summer begins. Mama said late in September when the north wind blows, the leaves start to turn, and the air is hazy. Daddy shook his head and argued that it's when the wind is still, the nights are cold, and the days are still warm. The only occurrence that the two could agree on concerning my favorite time of the year, was that Indian Summer always followed a hard frost.

In the fall of 1899, I was still dreaming about leaving our peaceful 41 acres for the bright lights of the big city. Mama always said that some people are never satisfied. Sometimes, I think she was referring to me. But I couldn't help it. I yearned for the bustling metropolis, where it was loud, scary and sometimes downright dangerous. The closest I'd ever been to a town where the stores had electric lights was Clinton, Missouri, which was ten or twelve miles west of the farm.

Once a month all the Truluck's, including Jerome and his flute, climbed aboard Daddy's hay wagon. With the mules, Satan and Angel, pulling the load we all sang along, while Jerome played, You've Been a Good Old Wagon But You Done Broke Down. How long the trek lasted depended on how high the creeks had risen overnight. Sometimes it took a half a day to reach Clinton. But that monthly adventure was still three weeks away, so I sought contentment under the lilac tree. It was a beautiful morning. The sun was shining, and the crows were cawing. I was inside my den, sprawled-out out on an old saddle blanket. As usual, I was barefoot, wearing a handsewn faded-green feed-sack dress with no sleeves. There was a definite smoky aroma in the air. I thought it might be our neighbor burning brush or maybe his log mill had caught on fire, again.

I peeked through the branches. There was Mama and Miss Linnie. The two women were gossiping and laughing while picking up fallen persimmons. Daddy and Jerome were down by the Tebo Creek catching dinner. I scooted further back in my hidey-hole. Sitting cross-legged, I pretended to be Chief Sitting Bull holding a pow-wow using a whittled hickory stick for my peace pipe. After holding the pipe up to the four directions, I gently put it down then picked up my most prized possession, and confidant, a rag doll named Ree Ree. Although she was a bit stained with age and ragged around the edges, in my eyes Ree Ree was as beautiful as a boxed doll. I tilted the large, blackened whiskey barrel bung, that served as her oversized head so I could look into Ree Ree's tiny white pearl button eyes.

Using my fingers to comb the doll's long black hair that had been cut from the tail of Angel, I said, "I haven't seen a butterfly in days. I think that's a sure sign that Indian Summer is here, don't you, Ree Ree?" Of course, there wasn't an answer from the lifeless doll with the limp body, but that fact didn't put an end to our one-way conversation. "I've been readin' that book, Uncle Tom's Cabin an' learnin' lots of important stuff. Like when Uncle Tom says, 'After ye've killed the body, there ain't no more ye can do. And there's all Eternity to come, after that'."

I swear on a good book that Ree Ree whispered, "Olivia, your memory is sharper than Mama Rose's". Now, that's not to insinuate that Mama minded me besting her when it came to reciting Bible passages. At an early age, that woman taught me and Jerome how to read. If we dogged the mule over a reading lesson, she always came back with, "You don't want to wind up a mudsill, now do you?" Meaning, living as an illiterate and uneducated Negro was a fate worse than slavery.

For a long time, I sat thinking about Eternity. Rocking back and forth on my rear end, I articulated my thoughts out loud. "I'll tell you something, Ree Ree, I'm not too sure about the kingdom to come. Brother Sin-Eater says God's realm awaits all those who believe in the resurrection of Jesus Christ. But coming back to life after a body's dead just doesn't fit in the natural order of things. Not to be sacrilegious, but that resurrection story is a little hard to swallow. Mama Rose says that a person's honest doubt in matters of faith is far better than those who are pious frauds. Come to think of it, Ree Ree, never once have I been witness to a dog, cat, or even Great Grand-Ma, Tillie Truluck, get up squawking after they'd already been put down for the eternal rest."

I sat under that lilac tree thinking so long and so hard about Eternity, that as the day slipped through the hourglass, I failed to notice that the slanting sun. Setting Ree Ree aside, I started to reach for my canteen, but first peeked through the branches. I was surprised to see Daddy and Jerome. Instead of walking, talking and laughing, like they usually did after a hard day of fishing, the two were running lickety-split across the field.

"Mama," Daddy hollered, between breaths. "Hurry. Get Olivia an' Miss Linnie to the root cellar."

I was even more surprised to see Mama drop all the persimmons she'd collected and start running for the root cellar, her white apron flapping in the breeze. Miss Linnie may have been an arthritic octogenarian, but on that day running behind Mama, her scrawny legs pumped up and down like they belonged to someone only four score.

"Olivia," Mama hollered. "Hurry, child. To the root cellar. Now."

I forgot about the water and plopped down on my rear-end. Scooting up against the smooth, thick trunk of the lilac tree, I asked myself, "What could be so important that Daddy would call all of us to the root cellar? A tornado? Couldn't be. There's not a cloud in the sky. Maybe this another one of his life lessons just to see how fast he can get all of us to jump up and run."

Tilting my head back, I looked up through a hole in the green foliage. High in the sky a lone black turkey vulture, wheeled in circles. "Maybe Daddy's not pulling a prank," I thought. "I could pull foot and beat it to the root cellar...but why? Indians? Not likely. The only Red Men left in Missouri are on Big Chief writing tablets." I remembered that a mountain lion had been seen in the area, prowling around Tebo Creek. "But Daddy wouldn't run from a big cat, would he? He'd use the breech loader." I rolled back on my haunches and figured by the time I broke cover and got my fanny to the root cellar, whatever was coming would already be here.

When I heard my name called again, I peeked through the branches. Daddy seemed to be miles away from the lilac tree. He had a hand cupped to his mouth, shouting, "Olivia. Olivia."

Then in the wink of my eye, Daddy was gone. There was nothing to be seen except a pile of hay covering the narrow door that was almost horizontal with the ground. That's when I heard the pounding of horses' hoofs. I scooted deeper into the protective arms of the lilac tree, held my breath, waiting until the sound stopped. When my 'Natural born curiosity' took control of my self-preservation, I slowly inched forward. When I peeked from between the lilac branches there were at least a dozen of them. Looking like mounted ghosts they wore white robes and hoods with eyeholes cut out of the fabric. I couldn't see their faces, but I didn't have to. I already knew the color of their skin. It was white as their sheets.

One of the men raised a flaming torch in the air, and hollered, "Come outta the house, Niggas."

Another hooded man on horseback screeched, "A'fore we burn it down wit' you'se in it."

In all my ten short years of living on God's green earth, I've never been so wrathy and scared at the same time. I pinched my arm to see if I was dreaming, but the unfolding scene wasn't some horrible nightmare. I just about swallowed my tongue when one of the men dismounted and headed toward my lilac tree. I froze stiff as an icicle and stopped breathing altogether, but dang-it, I kept my eyes open. The man came closer and closer. When he stopped, I was afraid he'd hear my heart pounding inside my chest. If I'd had the nerve I could've reached out with a stick and touched the toe of his boot. Thinking that the man could be Sam Hill, the Devil incarnate, I watched as he lifted his robe then whistled Dixie while watering the lilac tree. Luckily, I was well out of the line of fire. After finishing his business, the Ku Klux Klan man turned slowly, heading back to his horse. That's when I started breathing again, not normally, but enough that I didn't pass out. I'd always heard that white Missourians were known as pukes and now I knew the handle dang sure fit.

When I felt brave enough to raise my head and peek through the branches, two of the robed men holding torches moseyed up on our front porch. One of them kicked down the front door and disappeared inside. A few seconds later, orange flames were eating Mama's curtains. She'd saved her egg money for months to buy the necessary material. Then it took weeks of cutting and sewing. As the white gauzy Chantilly lace turned black, salty hot tears burned my eyes, blinding me. As they rolled down my cheeks, I remembered what Daddy had once told Mama, "Rose," he said, "your curtains make this house a home."

When gunfire erupted along with shouted profanities of the most horrible sort, my ears started to burn. The shooting and the loud boisterous guffaws made me want to scream, "Stop it." but I couldn't make a peep. Instead, I sank back against the tree trunk, shut my eyes tight and kept a fierce grip on Ree Ree.

****

"Olivia. Olivia, Dear. Wake up."

It was Mama Rose. She had managed to worm her upper body into my nest. Once I saw her the flood gates opened. I started bawling so hard my shoulders shuddered up and down. Mama always said that it wasn't real boo-hooing if there wasn't any snot coming out of a person's nose, and brother there was plenty of that. After I had cried my eyeballs out, she used her apron to wipe tear drippings from my chin and pulled me close to cuddle me up in her big strong arms. Humming my favorite hymn, All Things Bright and Beautiful, Mama rocked me back and forth.

When I'd settled down enough to quit sniveling, we crawled out from underneath the lilac tree. I couldn't hold it back and started boo-hooing again while staring at the charred rubble of our once beautiful home. The five of us must have been a pitiful-looking bunch, hoping this was a nightmare, but the grey puffs of smoke still drifting heavenward were stark reminders that this was reality. Mama rested her head on Daddy's shoulder. She wiped her nose and eyes with the corner of her apron and for the first time in my short life, I didn't see a smile on Mama's face.

"It's all gone," Mama moaned, slowly lifted her head to stare at Daddy. I'd never seen her look so peaked. Her voice was soft and low, and it cracked when she spoke. "Oh, Simon. Everything we've ever worked for. It's all gone. What will we do? What can we do?"

Daddy heaved a great big sigh. "One dad-blamed thing for sure, we'll have to hang up the fiddle on the 41 acres." There was that long moment of silence, then he whispered, "The gold, Rose. What about the gold?"

"Buried under the big flat rock behind the outhouse."

"Why, Daddy?" Jerome asked. My brother's smooth face was all twisted and funny looking. His eyes were red-rimmed, too. "Why'd they do this to us? We didn't do nothin' to them, did we?"

Daddy seemed to be having a hard time trying to explain the unexplainable, so Miss Linnie filled in the blanks. "Hate makes them white folks go crazy. You 'member that rabid skunk that showed up last year? He was all frothin' at the mouth, he was. Snappin' at anything that came near."

"I saw the hate today," I said. "It was in the man's eyes."

"But Daddy," Jerome whined. "You shot that skunk. You gonna' do the same to those white men? They're rabid, too, right?"

Daddy slowly shook his head from side to side. Even as strong as he was, with his broad shoulders and big hands, able to plow the fields from sunup to sundown without complaining, I'd never seen him so strung-out and down in the dumps as he was at that very moment. Speaking nary a word, he just stared at the charred embers. Daddy finally raised his head up to look at Jerome and me. His brown eyes were red and had turned watery. Up to the time, I didn't think grown men were allowed to cry, especially not my Daddy.

The man I loved so dearly cleared his throat as he looked at Mama. "We still got the old hay wagon. I'll find Satan and Angel. Those two couldn't have gone far. You stay with the young'uns." Daddy handed Mama the breechloader. "If those white Devils come back, use this if'n you have to."

Mama turned to me. "Olivia, you and Jerome gather up anything you can."

Miss Linnie was already using a stick to stir through a pile of smoldering ashes. "Olivia," she barked, "help me find my iron skillet. There ain't gonna' be no biscuits unless I got my cookware."

It was one of the few times in my life that I didn't immediately carry out Miss Linnie's orders. Instead, I reached up, pulled on Daddy's shirt, and begged, "Please, Daddy. I didn't mean it. I don't want to go to the city. We can't leave our home."

"What do you care about the farm?" Jerome asked, all smarmy

and know-it-all like. "All you've been talkin' about is sayin' good-bye to the Tebo forever."

"You be quiet, Jerome," I shot back, "and mind your own business."

"Both of you," Miss Linnie croaked. "Get to work."

Daddy bent over to get down eyeball to eyeball with me. "I'm sorry, Olivia. This is not our home anymore. We're not wanted here. We've got to leave."

"But where can we go?"

Daddy shrugged, stood up straighter and shook his head. "We'll talk to Brother Sin-Eater. Maybe he has an answer."

☐

CHAPTER THREE
BROTHER SIN-EATER

While Daddy rounded up Satan and Angel, the rest of us Trulucks tried our dead-level best to avoid the hot spots. Every time we stirred the ashes searching for any usable household items a small fire would flare up, again. Once everything salvageable had been recovered, even the blackened tintype of Gran-pappy Truluck, I made a beeline to the lilac tree, all the time thinking, "We're leaving the farm but where will we go? The city?" I stopped at the entrance to my hiding place, and asked, "Is this how my wish is to be granted? Our house gone? Burned down to the ground? But not everybody wanted to leave the 41 acres, just me." Once inside my den, I grabbed Ree-ree, the chalkboard and other collectables, hurriedly stuffing everything in an old hatbox. I couldn't stop mumbling over and over, "It's all my fault."

As I was crawling out from underneath the lilac tree's branches, Daddy called out, "Olivia, get over here and help with the mules. Satan and Angel are bein' ornery. Probably spooked by the gunfire."

When we finally had the two spiteful critters hitched to a hay wagon, I asked, "How long are we going to be gone, Daddy?"

He heaved a heavy washboard and wash-pan over the side and into the wagon, then shrugged. "Now, Olivia," he said, his rising voice an octave higher than normal. "I've done told you more than once. We've got to leave this place for good."

15

"But where are we going?"

"Stringbean, I ain't like that gypsy lady with the picture cards. I can't see into the future no more than the next minute, but look around, sure enough, there's nothin' left for us here but black ashes and white hate. We have to move on."

I shoved the hat box full of my most precious treasures in the rear of the wagon. All the talk about black and white made me puff my chest out, and huff, "Well, one thing for sure. It just don't seem right that all of us have to leave. I know, Daddy. Maybe you an' me could stay and the rest could go."

"One goes, we all go'es," Daddy replied.

"After all the work you and Mama put into this place. What a waste. Why...why, I could just kill those..."

"Olivia," Mama interrupted, then added. "There's nothing left of our home but cinders and memories. The only thing for us to do is to turn and leave."

I muttered a couple of "Gol' dangs" under my breath, then declared, "None of this seems right at all, at least not to me. I tell you, something oughta' be done. Daddy, why don't you get the sheriff."

"And tell him what?" Daddy asked. "That his brother-in-law burned down our house?"

Mama carefully placed her charred hand-carved wooden biscuit bowl and stirring spoon in the corner of the wagon, next to what little was left of her good China. She turned to look at me, and said, "Your Daddy's right, Olivia. We can't stay. No telling what would happen if those men came back and found us still here."

"Have faith, Stringbean," Daddy said, chuckling me under my chin. "There must be safer pastures for us elsewhere."

"But where?" Jerome asked, climbing onto the wagon with his flute in hand. "Where is it better than right here?"

Miss Linnie placed her foot on a wooden box, reached up with her good hand and grabbed the iron railing on the side of the wagon. She turned, looked at Jerome and cackled. "Don't you fret, Chil'. The Lord works in mysterious ways. He may taketh away but the Lord giveth back a hundred-fold to those who are just."

"And don't ever forget," Mama said, with a bit of warmth and humor returning to her voice, "When you come to the end of your rope – tie a knot and hang on."

****

Once the wagon had been loaded, Daddy strung a tarp over the front half of the bed as a cover to protect people and perishables from the elements. I squeezed my skinny body into a crack between Daddy and Mama up front on the hard-wooden seat. Jerome and Miss Linnie settled down on a singed goose-down quilt spread out under the tarp. Daddy clicked his tongue, and the two old mules lifted their hoofs like they weighed a ton and slowly started to move. The snapping sound of a long hickory switch with a leather strap tied on the end kept the snorting critters on the right path.

Daddy lit his corncob pipe and grumbled, "I'll be dad-blamed. Every mule, especially these two chuckleheads, thinks itself worthy to stand with the king's horses. Ain't that right, Stringbean?"

I nodded in silent support and rested my head against Mama's shoulder. I had no sooner closed my eyes and drifted off to dreamland when I was jarred awake by a loud thud.

"Wha's happened?" I asked, sitting up, trying to get my bearings.

"Nothing, Dear," Mama said. "We hit a hole."

"How much further?" I whined, not like Jerome would do, all high-pitched and nauseating, but with a pleasant hum.

"We're almost there," Mama said, then added one of her favorite chestnuts. "Remember, Olivia, the turtle who forever has to carry his house on his back goes slowly but gets just as far as the hare. He only takes a little longer to get there."

We rode on in silence for another mile or so. When lights from a house in the distance became apparent, I asked, "Mama, why is it that Brother Sin-Eater can't hear like other folks?"

Mama sighed, put an arm around my shoulders and pulled me closer. "Because, Olivia, when Brother Sin-Eater was a young boy in slavery, his master found out that his little slave could sniff out a covey of quail."

"And that's how he lost his hearing, pointing birds?"

Mama nodded. "Back during those terrible times, every slave went hungry. We never had enough to eat, only enough to keep us alive. Brother Sin-Eater was born with a talented nose. He could smell out quail, rabbits, turkeys – just about any wild creature you could imagine."

"I still don't see how..."

17

"When Brother Sin-Eater went on point, his master's gun went off so close to his ears that the sound made the child go practically stone cold deaf."

"Slavery," I hissed. The word was acid on my tongue. "That institution is not just peculiar, it's despicable. I wish it had never happened."

Mama chuckled and patted my bare knee. "Remember, Olivia, if wishes were horses, then beggars would ride instead of walk."

I sat quietly and stewed, thinking about how cruel masters used to be to their slaves, especially that Simon Legree in Uncle Tom's Cabin. That mean man flogged poor Uncle Tom to death. All the talk of people owning other people was getting me all riled up inside. Just thinking about the word 'slave' made my blood boil and smoke come out of my ears.

Reluctantly, I pulled away from Mama's warm embrace, I asked, "That's why Daddy talks like a hoarse bullfrog, because of the bad things that happened to him when he was a slave."

"Yes, Dear. Your Daddy picked a peach off a tree right under the master's wife's nose. He did it because he was hungry. When Daddy took a bite of that peach the woman put a chokehold on him that hurt something in his throat. That's why his voice is so deep and different sounding. Now, Olivia, stop all this talk about such disagreeable subjects and get some sleep."

****

This time, I laid my head on Mama Rose's lap and finally dozed off, that is until I heard Brother Sin-Eater shout, "Huzza. It's the Trulucks."

When my eyelids popped open and rolled up like a window shade, I looked over to see the sun just starting to peek over the horizon. Daddy reined-in the mules to a stuttering stop. Mama grunted as she slowly climbed down off the wagon. She brushed wrinkles from her soot-stained white apron then looked back at me.

"Olivia, get down off the wagon and help me rustle up some vittles."

It seemed obstinance toward my elders was becoming a habit. I ignored a direct order from Mama and scooted across the seat to bump up against Daddy. I was so hungry I could've eaten hardtack without the jam, but I was also a nosy ten-year-old, starving for a bit of news. Thankfully, Mama gave up the argument with her bull-headed daughter. Softly humming Onward Christian Soldiers, she marched to the back of the wagon.

To make sure I heard every word of the conversation between Daddy and Brother Sin-Eater, I cleaned all the wax out of my ears with my forefinger. The tall barrel-chested preacher who proudly claimed he once 'kilt' a bear with a hunting knife was wrapped in a white robe that was cinched around his waist with a black rope.

"Morning, Brother Sin-Eater," Daddy said, removing his wide-brim felt hat.

Brother Sin-Eater stood next to the wagon and shouted, "Morning, Brother Truluck. I take it you're here because of the recent burnings."

"We are," Daddy shouted, making sure his words were spoken directly into the long tin hearing-horn Brother Sin-Eater held up to his right ear. "Have there been others?"

"Over there." Brother Sin-Eater, lowered the hearing device to point toward a grove of maple trees. "There are more families whose homes have been burned to the ground. They all come to me looking for guidance. I've been down on my knees prayin' hard to the Lord to keep me up to the task."

"What about the state militia? Has anyone sent for help?"

Brother Sin-Eater shrugged. His long white beard rose off his chest a time or two. He looked up at Daddy and lowered his voice. "I'm afraid we're on our own." He pointed heavenward. "Help can only come from the One who resides up there."

"Even with God's help, where can we go?" Daddy asked.

Mama Rose, Miss Linnie and Jerome had all scooted to the front of the wagon. Mama handed Brother Sin-Eater a chunk of hardtack covered with strawberry jam, which he accepted in a most polite manner. After a brief silent prayer, the brush arbor minister consumed the offering in one big bite and never seemed to swallow.

Brown breadcrumbs and red jam glistened in his beard when Brother Sin-Eater lifted his tin horn in the air and declared, "I was hungry as a wolf but now I'm full and shall seek Divine intervention for those who come seeking help."

****

There was standing room only in the Church of the First Born. Brother Sin-Eater stood at the front of the congregation whose ages ranged from nine months to ninety. Holding the Holy Bible

19

high in the air, he shouted, "Brothers and Sisters, we've come here today to ask for the Lord's guidance. There are evil forces afoot who would not hesitate to rape, plunder and murder us. They've burned our homes and now the blood lust is on their tongues. Soon, it will be our necks in a noose. Our only hope is to flee – but where, oh, Lord? Yea, verily, that is the question – where can we go to find peace and safety? We beseech thee Lord to show us the way."

There was an enthusiastic round of "Alleluias" and "Amens", Mama Rose got infused with the Spirit and broke out singing Roll Jordon Roll. We all clapped our hands and sang along, not in one voice but with honest-to-goodness passion. With Jerome accompanying on the flute, what some of us lacked in musical ability, we more than made up in sheer volume.

When the singing and shouting had died down, Brother Sin-Eater held up the Holy Book high over his head. "When I talk privately with God, it's in a closet. But today, today we find ourselves in such dire straits that we've all come together to pray for guidance. So, what better place to start our conversation with our Heavenly Father, than with the Good Book?"

Brother Sin-Eater was not one to flip through the pages of the Bible, looking for a quick entrance or an easy exit. He opened his well-worn copy to the Book of Genesis. That's not to say he read it word for word. The story of Adam and Eve was told in Brother Sin-Eater's own words, leaving out the unimportant parts such what sort of leaf Adam wore and how Eve's hair hung down past her waist. He did elaborate on the unlimited bounty that was given to the first two humans of God's unique creations. When Satan first appeared, he was revealed as a friend intent on helping Adam, but later turned out to be an evil enemy by enticing Eve with the fruit of knowledge. I didn't think it possible, but at the end of Genesis, Brother Sin-Eater's loud voice increased in volume.

"Adam and Eve were banished from the Garden of Eden, cursed to spend the rest of their Earthly days in search of a way to return to the Lord. Beware brothers and sisters, it's much easier to give in to temptation and lose one's faith than it is to find it again."

By the end of the Tower of Babel passage, Brother Sin-Eater was shouting to the roof tops. "Man was an arrogant bug no better than a cocky roach. God saw this and made sure His creation spoke in different tongues, which in turn caused man to become confused and alienated from his own kind."

The moment of truth came when Brother Sin-Eater opened the Holy Bible to the Book of Exodus. He raised his wooly head to set his steel-gray eyes on the faithful before him. A bright light shone forth from his countenance, and the entire congregation, even Miss Linnie who last I'd checked was catnapping, sat perched on the edge of our seats, desperately waiting to hear a divine revelation.

Finally, Brother Sin-Eater pulled out an envelope that had been stuck between the pages of his Bible. He held the white missive up and called out, "Brothers and Sisters. This letter was sent to me from one of the faithful. In it he describes a new land, a land of milk and honey. Glory be, the Lord has shown me the way. We will trust in God to lead us to a new Promised Land. To a place where we can live without fear of harm and our children can run free."

After Brother Sin-Eater's rousing sermon, as the Truluck family slowly walked back to our wagon, I asked, "Mama, exactly where is this land of milk and honey?"

Mama stopped walking, turned to look at me straight in the eye, and replied, "Olivia, that's a good question. Some say it's where Moses led the Jews. But as for us? For us, it's anywhere out of misery.".

.

CHAPTER FOUR
HAIR SHIRT

That evening, as the Truluck family gathered around a campfire fueled with dried cow chips, we stuffed our bellies with Mama's skillet biscuits smothered in greasy cream gravy with a side helping of jimmy-crack-corn. After Daddy commented on the somewhat earthy flavor of the biscuits, he turned to Mama, and asked, "Well, Mother, do we follow Brother Sin-Eater and absquatulate for the land of milk and honey?"

"If you mean, do we take leave of this God-awful place, then the answer is yes."

Miss Linnie chimed in. "Some of the people here-abouts are all fired up, talkin' 'bout heading for the city. As for me, I ain't hankerin' to live where the cement grows. When my bare feet hit the ground, I want dirt to be between my toes."

Methodically, Daddy tapped the spent ashes from the bowl of his pipe into the glowing embers of our campfire. He shook his head. "I do wish them folks well," he said, "but the streets in Kansas City ain't exactly paved with gold."

"That's true, Simon." It was Mama making sure Jerome got the last biscuit. "But white folks always have a need for a maid or a handyman."

Daddy chuckled. "Guess if I can't get a job poundin' nails, I'll shovel horse manure or shine shoes."

Miss Linnie took a swig out of a little brown jug, made a

scrunched-up face, passed moonshine to Daddy, then cackled, "It don't surprise me one bit but what some will do to feed a hungry family. Why, to get an extra crust of bread, I used to pick the fleas off'n my massa's coon hound. Ten of them little critters got me half a biscuit." Miss Linnie had a distant look in her eyes as she continued to reminisce. "Now, that Clarion was a right stout ol' coon dog. The 'king of blue ticks', that's what my massa' called him. When the king was treed, you could hear his callin' clear across the valley and all the way to Sunday."

I held up my hand. When Daddy nodded in my direction, I asked, "If we go with Brother Sin-Eater will we be called refugees, immigrants, or the dispossessed?"

No one had an answer for my question, but after a unanimous Truluck vote of "Aye," our lot had been cast.

****

The next morning, after having said our sincere goodbyes to all those who were heading to the city, six wagons along with about fifty brave souls, put their faith in Brother Sin-Eater's revelation.

"We venture forth into the vast unknown wilderness," our leader shouted. "Let the trek began. Aim your wagon toward the west and a better life."

Daddy wasn't sure if our two mules could carry our load, so he traded old Satan, along with his good hunting knife and a sack of seed corn with no mold, for two oxen. They were hearty snorting beasts with the brain of a bug, but entirely capable of pulling our wagon. In a futile effort to snag a carrot tied to a stick, Angel clopped along behind, playing the role of caboose in our slow-moving train. Miss Linnie and Jerome made themselves comfortable spots to stretch out under the tarp. As for me, I squeezed into the crack I'd made between Daddy and Mama.

Thinking out loud, I scooted even closer to Mama, and asked, "Why didn't Daddy curse those men who burned our house?"

"What difference would that have made?" Mama answered. "Nothing Daddy could have said would have changed what they did."

Daddy must have had his ears perked. "That's right, Stringbean. What's done is done."

"And what's dead is dead," Mama mumbled. "And we'll leave it at that."

An hour later when the sun's rays started to burn the back of my neck, I asked, "How far is it to the Promised Land?"

Daddy flicked his hickory switch at a swaying black rump of the more stubborn oxen, and said, "All the way through Indian country and beyond, Stringbean."

It took a moment for that eye-opener to sink in. "Indians? Daddy, are you serious?"

"Sure am."

"Don't fret, child," Mama said, her voice soft and comforting. "Brother Sin-Eater says once we get through Oklahoma Territory it's clear sailing. Remember, he said that Monterey is a place in California where Negros can live in peace."

"Monterey, California. That must be a long way from Missouri. You mean we can live there without our home getting burned?"

"Yes, Dear," Mama whispered, stroking my cheek. "Without our home being burned."

"But the savages? They might take me and Jerome hostage? Well, probably not Jerome, he's too ug…"

"Olivia," Mama cut in. "You've been listening to your Daddy's balderdash way too much. Those stories he's been telling you and Jerome about blood-thirsty Indians are his made-up fabrications. What have I told you about believing nothing of what you hear?"

"But it was Daddy who told me," I mumbled.

Mama cupped my chin and looked me straight in the eyes. "The Red Man and the Black Man have both suffered at the hands of the white Man. Indians are the original people. Like you and me, they don't see a difference in the color of a person's skin. Native Americans treat everyone as if we were all created equal."

"Your Mama's right, Chil'." It was Miss Linnie who had scooted up to the front of the wagon. "Back in the old days them Indians had to pack up their bows and arrows. Just like us now, only instead of ridin' west they walked without much to eat."

"Only the Good Lord knows their suffering," Mama added, "or how many died. Lordy, Lordy it must have been terrible." Mama put her arm around my shoulders. "But they made it all the way to their Promised Land, and we will, too, but only if we persevere."

Miss Linnie cackled then leaned over the seat to whisper, "Just as long as Simon keeps a rein on those oxen and the cr'k don't rise."

****

I'm sure the Indians must have suffered mightily during their mass migration, but then again, so did yours truly. Not only had I spent the last two straight days bouncing up and down on a hard-wooden seat, but I was still wearing the hair shirt of guilt. I wanted to scream, "I didn't mean for all of us to leave the farm, just me." When it was time to stop for the night, instead of making my bed in the wagon, where Miss Linnie sang gospel hymns in her sleep, I curled up under a saddle blanket next to the glowing embers of our campfire. Even though I was bone tired, I couldn't fall asleep right away. Being a country girl, I was born in the woods and wasn't scared by a hoot owl, but on the trail, living in Mother Nature's bosom, I kept a sharp eye out for the dreaded million-legged centipede, nasty crawling critters that had poison in their tail and razor-sharp pinchers up front. I lay on my pallet listening to the night sounds and couldn't help but think about what we had left behind. I could only hope that one day, a girl about my age would find the secret hiding place and call it her home. If she turned out to be the daughter of one of the men who burned down our house, I wouldn't hold her any ill will. Mama always said that children should not be held responsible for their parents' evil deeds, but then again, Brother Sin-Eater was always talking about the sins of the fathers coming back to haunt the children. I took stock of my present situation and came to the comforting conclusion that we still had enough food to eat, a partial roof over our heads, and most important of all, we had each other. Besides, we were headed to Monterey, California. If the Indians could find a place to settle out West, so could we. Finally, with my eyelids heavy, I drifted off into slumberland thinking, "Just because I had a hankering to leave the farm maybe our house burning down wasn't exactly my fault. It might turn out to be a boon to the Truluck family."

****

It was on the fourth morning of our trek. The oxen had been hitched, a new carrot tied to Angel's stick, and I was in my regular place, sitting between Daddy and Mama. As usual I had a few questions. "Daddy, how will we know when we're in Indian Territory?"

"When we see the smoke signals, Stringbean."

"Simon, don't be teasing the girl. We'll know it when we get there, Dear."

I sat and stared straight ahead, then suddenly, without

25

provocation or warning, I started bawling. Mama lifted my chin with her thumb, and asked, "Good Lord, Olivia, what in the world is wrong?"

Once I was back in control of my emotions, I looked up at Mama all teary eyed, and said, "I'm sorry, Mama. I'm to blame for us having to leave the 41 acres. If I hadn't wanted to leave the farm, then none of this would have happened."

"Oh, Olivia. What on earth ever put a thought like that in your head? You had nothing to do with us leaving Missouri."

"That's right, Chil," Miss Linnie said. "You're just grievin' for what's been lost that's all. The onus ain't on you, it's on those men wearin' white sheets."

Mama wiped my eyes with her apron, pulled me close and stroked my hair, which had grown down past my shoulders. The thick strands were black as midnight with nary a curl. Mama said my mane was straight as an arrow because of Indian relatives on Daddy's side of the family. Even though I asked him many times, Daddy called that sort of talk bunkum, and never would admit having a drop of Redman blood running through his veins. I snuggled closer to Mama, resting assured that I was innocent of tempting the fates and that everything good or bad happened for a reason.

****

It was mid-afternoon when I stood up on the seat and pointed in the distance. "Look. A sign."

As we came closer, I read the faded words out loud. "Cheap Whiskey For Sale?" I turned to Daddy, and asked, "Why would anybody sell demon rum? Don't people in Joplin make it at home, like you?"

Daddy chuckled. "Because, Stringbean, there's folks who have a strong hankerin' for the anti-fogmatic but don't have skill to make it."

The farther we traveled, the rutted dirt road turned gummy from a recent rain and animal urine. More and more signs popped up advertising 'Cheap Rooms', 'Cold Beer', and a 'Shave with Haircut 2-Bits'. Everything was offered at 'Reasonable Prices'. When the wagon train came to a stop, Daddy reined-in the oxen.

"Where are we?" I asked.

"This is Joplin," Daddy said and spit a stream of black tobacco juice over the side of the wagon.

Wading through the muck, the bottom hem of Brother Sin-Eater's white robe had turned black with mud. He stood next to our wagon and announced, "We've arrived in Sodom."

I tugged on Daddy's arm. "But you said we're in Joplin, right?"

Brother Sin-Eater clarified his comment. "Sodom is every city. In Sodom, man's flesh is weak and the liquor flows like the mighty Miss-is-sip."

"Well, Brother Sin-Eater," Daddy shouted. "Makes no difference whether it's Sodom or Gomorrah. The front axle on this wagon is chatterin' like it's got the shiverin' chilblanes. We've got to find a blacksmith."

"Then we'll stop for repairs and rest the animals," Brother Sin-Eater announced. "And although, it's useless to preach God's word to the heathen, I will make an almighty effort."

As the wagons rolled closer and closer to Joplin, I felt a chill run up my spine. The Holy Bible said that Sodom was filled with sinners who turned a deaf ear to God's word. I couldn't help but feel sorry for the lost souls who were so arrogant, they didn't heed the Lord's teachings. I scooted closer to Mama Rose. She tucked me under her big strong arm and pulled me in close. I could hear her heart beating which gave me great comfort.

"Mama," I whispered. "If Brother Sin-Eater says we're supposed to pray alone in the closet by ourselves, then why is he going to preach on a street corner where everyone can hear him?"

"Brother Sin-Eater believes that a man warned is a man half saved. He believes it's his job to save all souls."

I thought about that for a moment then asked, "What's he saving them for? Christmas?"

"No, dear," Mama said, and gave me a strange look. "Sometimes Olivia, I do worry about you."

"Why's that, Mama?" I sat up straighter.

Mama looked at me and shook her head. "Here you are, ten-years-old, and you still haven't accepted Jesus Christ as your personal savior. I know you've got the inclination to be a skeptic, but you do understand, Olivia, that if you don't come to Jesus, you won't get through the pearly gates?"

I looked at Mama. Her ever present smile had evaporated. It seemed to me that since we left Missouri, Mama was smiling less and less. I wanted to make her lips turn up again, like they used to. If only I could say the right words. But the hard-cold truth was, how could I spout the platitudes of accepting Christ if they didn't ring true, at least in my heart? I sunk back in my seat, silently staring straight ahead.

"It's not my fault," I told myself. "Mama's the one who told me not to believe anything I hear. Now, she's all wrought-up over me not being a true believer. How can I believe in anything, if everything's a lie?".

CHAPTER FIVE
SODOM

As our wagon train crept closer and closer to the metropolis of Joplin, Missouri, we passed row after row of wooden buildings, most of which were unpainted, all looking like they'd been thrown together in one day and nailed to each other for mutual support. Pasted to a window or a door in big letters were signs that read 'Whites Only'. In the Western sky the sun was a big orang ball sitting on the horizon. When we crested a hill, shimmering in the distance were hundreds of bright twinkling lights.

"Is that Joplin, yonder?" I asked,

"Yes, Dear One," Mama answered.

"Whoa," Daddy barked. He reined in the oxen then pointed to the right. "Stringbean, my eyes are givin' out in the dark, read what's on that sign-board."

"Blacksmith. Negros Welcome."

Daddy tied the reins to the brake handle, climbed down off the wagon and walked over toward the blacksmith's shop where he spent a lengthy period of time jawboning with a huge muscular man wearing a black leather apron.

When Daddy came walking back to where we were all anxiously waiting for a report, he looked up at Mama. "The Smithy says he'll fix the axle for some of your canned beets and a peach cobbler. He'll let us camp behind his shop for fifty cents a night – that's per wagon."

I was sure glad to see a grin on Mama's face. "Good thing we cleaned out the root cellar," she said. "I've got plenty of canned goods." She pointed to a grove of peach trees by the side of the blacksmith's shop. "His cobbler will have to wait until Olivia and Jerome pick me some peaches."

****

As the wagon train formed a tight circle in the campground, Jerome and I gathered a half bushel of ripe peaches for the blacksmith's cobbler. I held up the kerosene lantern so that the light shined in his peachy-stained face. "I'm warning you, Jerome. You eat too many an' you'll get the skitters."

That evening, Mama baked two pies in her cast iron skillets, one for us and one for the smithy, then fixed a dinner of unleavened cornbread along with dandelion greens boiled with hog maws. We stuffed our bellies, until I thought mine might pop, then Jerome and I found a loafing shed to spend the night. Old saddle blankets protected our bare skin from the itchy hay, and we used wadded-up feed sacks as pillows. Once we had settled in, I laid back to look up at the night sky through cracks in the shed's thatched roof.

I was imagining how beautiful it must be in Monterey, California, when Jerome whispered, "Olivia?"

"What, Jer-ome?"

"Are you thinkin' about the heathens in Sodom...I mean, Joplin?"

"Why should I be? Mama says that except for ignoring the Word of God, they're no different that you and me."

"But Brother Sin-Eater says that..."

"Shhhh," I hissed. "Be quiet. Listen."

The sound of someone playing a piano drifted across the campground. Jerome sat up straight, and said, "I've never heard nobody play like that."

"Yeah," I drawled. "He's got it all fired up."

The musical notes came so fast that I wondered if the piano virtuoso had three hands and fifteen fingers. Jerome pulled out his hand-carved wooden flute that Daddy had given to him the previous Christmas. I was amazed how well he could almost keep up with the piano's syncopated rhythm.

I rose to a sitting position. "I bet the music's comin' from that roadhouse at the far end of the campground."

"What's a rode house? Is that a place where they ride

horses?"

"No, you dummy. Not r-o-d-e. R-o-a-d house. Mama told me never to go near one."

Jerome rolled his eyes at me. When he scratched his head there was a funny look on his face. "Why? Do the Sodomites live there?"

By this time, I'd lost whatever little patience I had left with my brother. A heavy sigh escaped my lips. "No, Jerome. What I mean is like I already told you. Joplin's heathens are just like you and me, except they can't admit the error of their ways." I jumped to my feet, dusted the hay from my feed sack dress and looked down at the knucklehead thing I called brother. "Well, are you coming or not?"

Jerome stood up on tiptoes to look me square in the eyes. "Okay, I'll go, but if I get Sodomized, it's gonna' be your fault."

By the light of the crescent moon, Jerome and I tiptoed across the campground until we were huddled up against the back wall of the roadhouse. I put a forefinger to my lips and with Jerome breathing down my neck and walking on my heels, we snuck around the side of the frame shack until we were squatting underneath an open window. We slowly raised our heads up until we could peek over the windowsill.

In all my ten years of spending time on God's green earth, I'd never seen such strange going-ons. A heavy cloud of smoke filled the room. I thought maybe the place had caught on fire, but if it had, nobody inside seemed to notice. Several Negro men lounged around a table, each with a big fat cigar stuck in his mouth. The smallest one had an Arkansas toothpick strapped to his hip with the long steel blade hanging all the way down to his knee. It was evident by the broad smile on everyone's face, the had left all their worldly problems outside the roadhouse.

Shelves lining one wall were packed with mason jars. The glass containers were filled with a clear liquid, the same kind I'd seen at Doc Moore's Traveling Medicine Show. The famous Doc from Texas sold every kind of patent medicine known to man. Each was for a different human ailment, from scurvy to fungal infections and fevers. Judging by the sheer quantity of patent medicine bottles lining the shelves in the roadhouse, I figured that most of the citizens living in Joplin, Missouri were of ill health due to their debased, sinful way of living.

Several of the roadhouse patrons were leaning on a waist-high bar, all laughing out loud with uproarious hoots and hollers, like maybe somebody had told one of those dirty jokes I'd heard about, but never actually heard in person. My mouth dropped plumb open when some of the men and women started dancing, right up against each other, so close there wasn't a crack left between them to let the tiniest ray of light shine through. A tall woman, her skin blacker than coal, stood on the sidelines with her foot propped up on a chair with her skirt pulled way up past her knee. The woman who Mama would call a "hussy" wore silk stockings, smoked a cigarette, sang and played a guitar, all at the same time, which made me wonder how she managed to breathe.

Suddenly, I felt tugging on my arm. "Olivia," Jerome whispered. "We better skedaddle, 'fore we get found out."

When the two of us were back in the loafing shed, Jerome plopped down on his saddle blanket and immediately fell asleep. All the excitement must have been too much for the little guy, but the uninhibited exhibition of joy that I'd just witnessed, made me yearn to participate. Then I remembered what Brother Sin-Eater had told us, "Except during times of procreation, men and women should keep a social distance of at least three-feet." I figured Brother Sin-Eater's gospel hadn't reached the corrupted sinners of Joplin, Missouri. On the other hand, there they were, people of my own color, dancing the night away, up close and personal. I lay on my saddle blanket, smiling and thinking, "Maybe this Joplin isn't such a bad place after all. Maybe our wagon broke down at this particular geographical location because it was supposed to. Maybe this is the Promised Land."

****

Early the next morning, Mama Rose came into the loafing shed shouting louder than Brother Sin-Eater during a Sunday sermon. "Olivia. Jerome. Time to rise and shine."

I popped up and had a good stretch. Jerome was lying in a fetal position. Usually, my brother was the first one out of the sack in the morning, meaning he'd be the first to claim a breakfast of whatever was left over from dinner the night before.

"Jerome," I hissed, prodding his rear-end with the toe my foot. "Get up an' get to walkin', hear?"

Mama looked down at me and asked, "Olivia, why is your brother still laying there? Is he sick?"

I shrugged, shook my head and mumbled, "I dun'no, Mama."

Mama bent over and placed her hand on Jerome's brow. "This boy's burning up. Jerome, baby," Mama begged, wiping the sweat from his face with her apron. "It's Mama. What's wrong with you?"

Jerome uncurled and let out a moan. He rolled over on his back, covered his eyes and pointed at his throat, then moaned again, and shut his eyes.

Mama straightened up and sighed. "It's his tonsils, again. And I'm all out of the medicine. It went up in the fire."

"Mama," I said, "I know where there's lots of medicine. The kind Doc Moore used to sell."

"Where, Dear?" Mama asked, a look of relief crossing her face.

"Over there at the roadhouse," I said, pointing toward the roadhouse. "They've got bottles and bottles of the cure sitting on the shelf."

Mama gave me a questioning look. "Oh, really, Olivia? And just how do we know all this, Missy?"

I shrugged and slowly drew out my words of explanation. "Well, last night, I heard music, an' it was goin' so fast, even Jerome couldn't keep up on his flute. So, him and me, we went an' peeked inside, just to see what was goin' on."

"And what did you see?" Mama asked.

I shrugged, again. I'd been in these tight spots with Mama before and I didn't want to lie. It occurred to me that my best defense against further questioning was to stick with the issue at hand. "Mama, Jerome's really sick. We've got to get him some feel-good medicine. Besides, I was only trying to help."

Much to my relief, Mama's frown softened. "I appreciate your concern, Olivia, but next time, before you decide to spy on something that's none of your business, remember, that's how the cat lost its tail."

By this time Daddy had come over to the loafing shed. He picked up his son like the boy was light as a feather and carried Jerome back to the wagon, while Mama and I followed. It seemed the Truluck's might be staying in Joplin longer than anyone anticipated.

****

While Miss Linnie kept Jerome cool with a wet cloth, Daddy supervised the axle repair, and I took shanks' mare to Joplin with Mama. On the way, she asked, "Olivia, what do you think is in those bottles at the roadhouse?"

"Medicine?"

Mama chuckled. "Dear, that place is a bucket shop where they sell beer and corn squeezins'. None of which will cure Jerome's aching throat. What we need is a bottle of Missus Winslow's Soothing Syrup."

From memory, I repeated what I'd read on the side of a bottle of Miss Winslow's. "'Made from the finest cocaine and guaranteed to cure everything that ails a person'."

Mama and I hiked over hill and dale, ignoring several 'NO TRESPASS' signs. When we were standing on the corner of Fourth Street and Main in Joplin, I had to crane my head to see the tops of the tall three-story buildings. My mouth hung open like a turkey in a rainstorm. And the people. I'd never seen so many men and women going in all different directions while carrying-on in such a strange fashion. It crossed my mind that "If this is the big city, I'm willing to give it a shot."

I grabbed Mama's arm, pointed down the street, and yelled, "Look. It's a wagon that runs without horses."

Mama stood stiffer than a wooden cigar-store Indian. "That's a streetcar, Olivia. It runs on electricity."

"Look at all those folks crammed inside. How does a person breathe all cooped-up like that?"

Electrical sparks cascaded overhead. The streetcar clanged its bell and with much screeching and grinding, finally turned the corner. Mama grabbed my hand. "Run, Olivia," she shouted, and practically drug me across the street.

We were almost to the other side, when a horseless carriage came barreling right at us going full chisel. The driver wore googles and a long black overcoat. He was perched high on the gasoline-powered contraption, screaming, "Make a hole. I can't stop." Mama and I jumped to the side. The horseless carriage roared past making strange 'Ah-oo-ga' sounds.

When Mama and I were safely standing on the wooden sidewalk, I cackled, "That tin-lizzie sounds worse than a ruptured bull."

Mama didn't crack a grin. She kept a super tight grip on my wrist and shook her head. "Olivia, I'm warnin' you. Stay away from those new-fangled gasoline contraptions. They're nothin' but trouble."

"With a capital T, Mama?"

"Don't get smart with me, Child," Mama huffed, squeezing my fingers even tighter.

We walked along the street staying in the shade of the Club Saloon, a huge two-story building with a sign covering the entire top floor, advertising Chancellor Cigars. One more block and it was our good fortune to find a drugstore that catered to Negros. When we stepped inside, I was transported to a storybook land filled with everything any ten-year-old girl could possibly need or ever want. Even though it was a good two months before sitting down to a Thanksgiving turkey, a Christmas tree held a place of prominence in the middle of the store. Mama had to drag me past the life-size dolls that looked so real I wanted to pick one up, throw it over my shoulder and give her a burp. Then I thought about my poor little Ree Ree and how I'd never give her up for a hundred dolls with white skin.

When we exited the drugstore, all I had to show for the entire experience was a thick piece of penny licorice. Mama clutched a bag holding a bottle of Missus Winslow's in one hand and my hand in the other. When we came to a cross street a raggedy-looking man came up to Mama and begged, "Pardon me Ma'am, but could you spare a dime?"

In a day filled with rude awakenings, the biggest shock came when I looked at the beggar. The man's skin was lily white, except in places where it was dotted with tiny black spots. In addition to a long hawk-like nose, the pitiful creature had scraggly blonde hair that hung to his shoulders and intense piercing blue eyes that seemed to look right through me. I couldn't decide if he was a fallen angel or the ghost of Christmas past.

CHAPTER SIX
READING, WRITING AND 'RITHMATIC

I'm loath to admit that when I was ten years old, I was dead-set prejudiced against white people – not that I'd ever known one personally to make such a critical judgement. I mostly didn't pay attention to light-skin folks, not because they were white, but because I just liked Colored. That's why it certainly was a shock to my system to be standing on a sidewalk in downtown Joplin, Missouri, in full public view, talking to a white man, who was pan-handling my Mama. I'd read enough yellow journalism to suspect it was a con, a ruse to kidnap a young Negro girl for the Chinese slave trade.

Mama eyeballed the man and slowly shook her head. "If I spare you a dime," she scolded. "You'd waste it on John barley corn. Am I not right?"

"No, Ma'am you're not. I swear," the man said, raising his right hand like he was taking an oath. "I'm saving my coins to escape this sinful city where leisure pastimes are entered into with unbridled wantonness. There's nothing here but dance halls, opium dens, billiard rooms that spew their filth hither and yon. Why, if you don't believe me just look down at your feet." Mama and I looked down to see that we were standing in puddles of expectorated black tobacco juice. The strange white man pointed toward Club Saloon. "And in the gutter."

We turned to see a grown white man down on his hands and

knees scrounging for cigar butts, sucking the last few drops from a liquor bottle.

"A terrible sight, I admit," Mama said. "But I'm sorry, Mister. You see my son is ill and we're in a hurry. And really, I don't have a dime to spare."

"Please, Ma'am," the man pleaded. "Is there any way you can help me?"

Mama eyeballed the man, then asked, "What name do you go by?"

"Horace G. Greeley, but I'm known as Swede. I'm a schoolteacher by trade."

Mama sighed and gave the man a nod. "Alright, Mister Swede. You look like you'd be able to carry your load, once I fatten you up and put some meat on your bones. Like I said, I don't have a dime to spare." Mama looked down at me, then up to Mister Swede. "You say you're a schoolteacher." Mister Swede nodded. "Then you can tutor my two children."

"Oh, how I thank you, Ma'am," Mister Swede, cried and took the beat-up cap off his head. Now that was the first time in my life that I'd seen a white man doff his hat to a Negro woman. Mister Swede twisted the cap into a knot and looked directly at me. "Ah, children. They're little brains are filled with such mush. I bet this one's a regular church bell."

Mama chuckled and shook her head. "Talkative, yes, but smart as a whip. Why this girl can read a book this thick," Mama held her thumb and forefinger an inch apart, "then recite it back to you word for word like she was a parrot."

Mister Swede nodded his head vigorously. "Yes, yes, she's been blessed with a photographic memory. But children need a good schooling to combat ignorance. As Aristotle once remarked, "The roots of education are bitter, but the fruit is sweet." Finally, Mister Swede turned his attention back to Mama. "Thank you, thank you, again, Missus…ah?"

"Truluck. Rose Truluck." Mama patted the top of my head. "And this is my daughter, Olivia."

Without further introductions, the three of us hurried out of downtown Joplin. When we came to the three-story brick mansion with a large "NO TRESPASS" sign out front, Mama forged straight ahead with nary a hesitation.

We were halfway across the smooth green lawn when someone

hollered, "Pa. There's niggas trespassin' on our property."

"Run," Swede hollered.

"Boom."

Up to that point in time, never once had I been threatened with bow and arrow, slingshot, or a gun. Now, with buckshot flying overhead, I hung onto the back of Mama's dress. My feet didn't touch the ground as we high-tailed-it toward the tree line. By the time we'd reached the woods, I'd firmly decided that I'd rather take my chances in Indian Territory than stay in Joplin where Negros are shot at like sitting ducks in a penny arcade.

****

Two days later, after consuming half a bottle of Miss Winslow's, Jerome's fever broke. I suppose his speedy recovery was due to a healthy immune system, rather than a cocaine-infused patent medicine that did relieve the pain of acute tonsillitis. We were back on the trail, again. This time, instead of a rutted dirt path, long wooden planks covered the rutted road. Daddy complained about the high cost of a toll road, but Mama said the pennies spent were a cheap price to pay for the way her rear end felt at the end of a long day's ride in a buckboard that was all board and nothing but buck.

Daddy kept the two beasts moving forward, while Mama sat up front to keep an eye out for danger. Miss Linnie and Jerome occupied a narrow place under the tarp, while Mister Swede and I sat with our legs hanging off the back of the wagon. I really didn't mind looking back to where I'd been. Sometimes, to see everything going in reverse is more entertaining than watching the scenery creep by you. Besides, I was more than happy just to leave the sin city of Joplin back in the dust where it belonged.

Except for the perpetual squeaking of a wagon wheel, the time-labored huffing of the oxen and a red-tailed hawk arguing with her mate, all was peaceful and quiet in my world, until suddenly, Mister Swede turned toward me and started yakking in my ear.

"Olivia, I promised your mother that I would be responsible for furthering your intellectual pursuits. Jerome, who is male, has different educational needs and will be taught separately. I hear you can read quite well. Is that correct?" Mama always warned me not to toot my own horn, so I shrugged without answering and nodded. "All right then. Let's see, where to start?" Mister Swede picked up his frayed knapsack and set it between us. In a low voice

that can only be described as melancholy, he whispered, "Everything I own of any value is in here. It's all that I have left since that terrible day in Saint Louis."

"Did you get burned out, too, Mister Swede?"

"No, dear Olivia, I was run out...but not before I was tarred, feathered and batty-fanged." I gave Mister Swede a questioning look. He smiled, and said, "Meaning, I was thoroughly thrashed." He pointed at dark black dots on his forearm. "Tar is difficult if not impossible to remove. The only thing that works is kerosene, but it burns the skin like all get out."

"Why would anyone tar and feather you?"

Mister Swede hung his head, which caused the blonde curly locks of hair to fall over his brow. He finally looked up at me, but with a face so sad it made me want to cry. "We were going to start the lesson today with McGuffey," he said, "but I suppose an education in human ethics should supersede book reading. Why was I run out of town on a rail?" He looked at me for a moment then shook his head back and forth. "You see, Olivia, my friends in St. Louis requested my humble opinion on Christianity, and I had the temerity to suggest that today's Christian identity is not a true expression of what it means to follow Jesus Christ. I spoke truth to power out loud, asking how my fellow Christians can live with their blatant hypocrisy? My naïve criticism came shortly after a Negro in Saint Louis was lynched by so-called Christians for stealing a beaver coat in the dead of winter. Of course, it's wrong to take a shopkeeper's possessions without paying, but without proper covering that man most likely would have frozen to death on the mean streets. When I asked my friends, 'Which do we value most, a yard or two of fur or a man's life'? Instead of honest answers, I got mean stares." Mister Swede sighed and slowly opened the knapsack's flap. "The only things of any worth I was able to save upon leaving Saint Louis were my books." He reached inside the bag and after finding what he was searching for, held it up. "This is the New England Primer, which is sometimes referred to as the Little Bible of New England." After opening the Primer to the first page, Mister Swede held it in front of me and nodded. "Read the first line out loud, please."

"Give ear my children to my words."

"Very good, Olivia. Now, read the rest of the stanza."

After I'd finished reading the short verse, which was now in my

memory banks forever, Mister Swede nodded his approval, closed the book, then turned to me. He pulled a small square tin box out of the knapsack, took a pinch of snuff between thumb and forefinger, held it to his nostril and with a mighty sniff, inhaled the tobacco. After repeating the same process in his other nostril, Mister Swede kept sniffing and sniffing. He couldn't seem to stop. I thought the poor man was going to keelhaul himself right out of the wagon. Finally, he snorted a mighty sneeze then pulled a red bandana from his pocket. I'd never before heard the mournful moan from a ship's foghorn, that is, until my tutor blew his nose. Satisfied that he'd expectorated all the unhealthy vapors that were tickling his nasal passages, Mister Swede sat up straighter and started another lecture on the fine art of what he referred to as "intellectual pursuits."

"Olivia my dear, Ethics are the soul of learning. The further you read into the Primer the more you'll find that the stern lessons within will help you navigate the rough shoals of life. There is no easy road to knowledge nor to salvation. Keep your nose to the grindstone, dear girl. and you'll grow from an unregenerate youth to a responsible contributing member of society. Now, to further your reading skills, we shall use McGuffey's Eclectic Primer and the American Spelling Book. Today though, we'll save those tomes of elucidation for a later time and delve into the preciseness of mathematics by opening to the first page of Normal Mental Arithmetic."

****

For the next few days, I could be found sitting cross-legged at Mister Swede's knee. At the end of every lesson, my tutor never failed to mention, "Little minds have a lot to learn to get big." My photographic memory easily absorbed the formal education, especially when it came to learning a new language such as Latin.

It was one balmy evening when our small wagon train stopped for the night. All of us Trulucks were huddled around a campfire. I was displaying my new-found knowledge of Latin by reading from Ahn's First Latin Book. I had just got to the difficult part, where the consonant stems have the same forms in all the genders, except that in the accusative singular, and in the nominative, accusative and vocative...when Brother Sin-Eater appeared from out of the shadows.

"Good evening, Trulucks," he declared and bowed at the waist.

In unison, all replied in a loud voice, "Good evening, Brother Sin-Eater."

"Huzzah, huzzah. Tomorrow we cross into Indian Territory. So far, God has helped us leave a spiteful Missouri behind. The Lord points the way but it's up to us to pray for His guidance and read His sign. Tonight, when you're alone, ask Him to protect and keep us from harm."

Again, in unison, we all hummed, "Amen."

As Daddy conferred with Brother Sin-Eater in private, Mister Swede turned to Mama. "Miss Rose, if you don't mind me asking...just where are you headed?"

"Monterey, California," Mama said, bending over to light a taper. Holding the flame to Daddy's corncob pipe, she gave it a couple of puffs, then shook her head. "Brother Sin-Eater tells us it's land that sits by the ocean."

"It does," Mister Swede said. "But the coastline is rugged, and the only source of income is fishing. Is that what your plans are, Missus Truluck, to try your luck at hauling in sardines and mackerel?" Mama nodded her head. "I beg your pardon, Miss Rose, but where I come from the old expression 'don't sell me a dog' might apply."

Mama silently puffed on her pipe a long time. Finally, she said, "Four of the twelve apostles were fishermen. If that's what it takes to feed my family, then I'll cast a net in the water, too.".

CHAPTER SEVEN
LITTLE AFRICA

One butt-numbing, leg aching week had passed since our wagon train crossed over the Missouri state line and now, we were knee-deep into Indian country where we celebrated Jerome's eighth birthday. That evening everyone stood with fork in hand, waiting for a piece of Mama's flat cake covered with white icing made from real cane sugar, instead of blackstrap molasses. After the birthday celebration, Mama and I were washing dishes. One of the men in the wagon train came over to have a word with Daddy. Now I'm not a naturally nosy person but I did manage to turn my K. P. task over to Jerome, the child was so easy to direct, and slipped away into the dark night. Quiet as a mouse, I crawled under the wagon and slowly inched closer to where the two men were jaw boning.

"I tell you, Simon," the man hissed. "It just don't seem right to me. After all the miserable days we've spent on the road, not to mention the fact that one of my oxen has gone lame, an' we still ain't much closer to the Promised Land than we was when we first started."

"We-ll, Winston," Daddy said, drawing out the w-e-l-l like he sometimes did when he was in serious conversation. "Today, we made over twenty miles, not takin' into account the two-mile detour."

"What I want to know," the burly man huffed, "why haven't we seen a sign, from God?"

Daddy offered, "Probably because we're still a long way from Monterey."

"I tell you one thing fer sure, if'n Brother Sin-Eater don't put an end to this senseless wanderin', pretty soon I will. Look around. This is some right pur'ty country we've been passin' through. Good flat land with sandy soil. Why, I bet we could grow bumper crops of wheat and corn. Sometimes I think Brother Sin-Eater's got us goin' around in circles, sorry, but I do."

"I don't disagree with what you're sayin', Mister Winston." Daddy knocked his corncob pipe on the wagon wheel. Hot ashes rained down on my head. Suffering in silence, I kept my lips zipped as he continued. "Tell the truth, I'm gettin' plumb tired of this journey, too. But before we left Missouri, all of us agreed to keep on goin' until Brother Sin-Eater tells us to stop. A promise is a promise, ain't that right?"

Mister Winston kicked the ground with the toe of his boot. "The weather's turning cooler and the leaves are startin' to change. If we don't stop soon, winter will fall on us and we'll all freeze to death. You realize to get to California we've got to pass through New Mexico then Arizona? I say we take a vote an' settle this hash. Who wants to stay and who wants to keep goin' on. That's the democratic way to solve things, ain't it?"

"I agree, Mister Winston. If there are those who vote to stake their claim here, then I say stay and prosper. God speed to the rest."

Once the man had left, I crab crawled backward from underneath the wagon and innocently leaned against Daddy's stout leg. He placed a loving hand gently on my head, and asked, "Stringbean, you been eves-droppin' on Daddy, again, huh?"

I couldn't argue the point by saying "no" without lying, so I asked, "You think Mister Winston is right, Daddy? Instead of goin' to Monterey, we should stay here, in Indian Territory?"

Like I was his favorite pet, Daddy stroked my hair, before he replied, "Whether we go or stay, I think we'll leave it up to God and Mama Rose."

****

The next morning, instead of breaking camp at sunrise, as we usually did, everyone gathered around Brother Sin-Eater's wagon. It was the moment of truth. I admit, our situation wasn't as desperate as those brave men who fought and died at the Alamo.

There weren't thousands of Mexican soldiers lusting for our blood, only the KKK. I was sort of disappointed though that Brother Sin-Eater didn't draw a line in the sand. Instead, we took a vote. Those who wanted to stay in the Oklahoma Territory made their decision known by raising their hands.

After the voting, I helped Daddy hitch-up the oxen. Once we were on the road again headed toward the Promised Land, Mister Swede and I assumed our usual positions toward the back of the wagon. I sat cross-legged with my small chalk board resting on my lap, waiting for my tutor to assign the next arithmetic problem.

"Olivia, please divide two-hundred-ninety-six by seventy-four."

When I had the right amount calculated inside my head and written down, I turned the board toward Mister Swede.

He looked down his long straight nose at my answer, then at me. "But where is your division work?"

"Right up here," I said, pointing to my head.

"Olivia, your innate intelligence would make a stuffed bird sing."

I knew Mister Swede meant that most people would think it absolutely preposterous, that when it came to arithmetic a ten-year-old Negro girl was so dang fast with numbers she could do problems in her head. But at that particular moment, I had something else on my mind besides math.

"Mister Swede. This morning, when some voted not to follow Brother Sin-Eater – does that mean they've lost their faith in God to guide them to the Promised Land?"

When he shook his head, my tutor's long stringy blonde hair fluttered in the breeze. "No, Olivia. It means they've lost their trust in Brother Sin-Eater. I might ask though, just who is this Sin-Eater fellow, and what makes him the biggest toad in the puddle?

I had to ponder that question long and hard before replying. "Brother Sin-Eater says he's a direct conduit to the Almighty. But…lately, I've been thinking about something Mama told me a long time ago - about believing none of what I hear." I looked at Mister Swede and patted the arithmetic book in his hand. "Mathematics is believable and understandable. The answers are constant. Two plus two always equals four. Numbers never lie, do they, Mister Swede?"

Mister Swede chuckled. "Only if used by accountants and bankers. Now, back to the business at hand, Olivia. I want you to divide nine-hundred-fifty, by…Olivia, are you not writing on your chalk board today?"

"We-ll," I said, drawing the word out like Daddy and laying the chalk down. "I've been thinking, again."

"Oh-oh," Mister Swede grumbled, closing the arithmetic book and placing it on his lap. "Judging by your recent progress, I suppose math can wait. And your Mama's right. Don't believe anything that you hear, unless you verify it with known facts. Now, Olivia, what else is on your mind, today?"

"This morning, all the men got to vote go or stay, right?" Mister Swede silently nodded. "Why not the women?"

"Well, I…"

"In this wagon train is it just all men are created equal? What about the women? Are they nothing but scullery maids without a voice? If that's the case then pardon me, I'm…I'm…ah, Mister Swede, what do you call someone who's very confused?"

"Fifteen puzzled."

"Yes, that's it. I'm fifteen puzzled."

Mister Swede cleared his throat, and said, "Since you asked, Olivia, I believe in one person, one vote, no matter their sex, the color of their skin or if they're fifteen puzzled."

Suddenly, Mama's voice came from close by. "Did I just hear you right? Give women and Negros the vote? Why, no wonder they tarred and feathered you in St. Louie." I turned my head to see Mama holding a water canteen. "Mister Swede," she declared. "Be careful of what you're doing. Putting radical ideas such as 'suffrage for all' inside this child's head, why that could lead to unintended consequences way beyond our control."

Mister Swede graciously accepted the canteen from Mama. He took a long swallow of water then said, "Missus Truluck, no matter if they're short or tall, black, brown or red, suffrage is a universal right for all American citizens. To deny such a large majority of the population based on their sex, creed or color, is overt discrimination. I've read that change is in the air. Why, who knows, I wouldn't be surprised if one day this country had a Negro in the U. S. Congress."

"I wouldn't hold by breath," Mama huffed and turned away to return to the front of the wagon.

****

For another few days we kept trekking West, until the morning of

45

September 31st, 1899. I was riding up front with Daddy and Mister Swede. Mama, Miss Linnie and Jerome were at the back of the wagon, plucking feathers off the chicken that would be the Truluck's dinner. Suddenly, without forewarning, Mister Swede leapt to his feet. Leaning forward like he was ready to mount one of the oxen, he pointed to a sign in the distance. I stood up, leaned forward and squinted hard.

"Huzzah," Mister Swede shouted. "We're here."

Daddy kept the wagon moving until we drew even with the sign. He reined-in the oxen by the side of the road, and asked, "Where?"

Miss Linnie surfaced to ask, "Are we in the Promised Land yet? The bones in my rear-end tell me so."

"Mister Swede seems to think so," I said, looking at the exuberant expression coloring the man's normally serious white countenance.

There came a commotion from up front of the wagon train. Then, Brother Sin-Eater came marching toward our wagon. As he came closer there was fire in the preacher's eyes.

Brother Sin-Eater cried out, "Who says we stop here?"

Daddy nodded toward Mister Swede. "The gent says we're here."

"What's that? Brother Truluck, are you putting your faith in that tarred coot?"

Daddy kept the answer to himself. I turned toward the whitewashed wooden plank sticking out of the ground, and read the one word out loud, "Tulsa?"

Mama stood behind Daddy and asked, "Are we really dropping anchor here, Simon?"

Everybody, including Brother Sin-Eater, held their breath. Daddy turned to look at Mister Swede, who now stood at attention, sort of in the manner of Christopher Columbus when he shouted, 'Land ho'. Brother Sin-Eater kept his trap shut but still wore the scowl of an angry Old Testament prophet.

Finally, Daddy broke the silence. "Brother Sin-Eater," he said, his voice soft and low. "Truth be told we surely do appreciate all the things you've done for us. If'n it weren't for you, we'd still be back in misery. But I believe this is where we part company. It's not that I don't respect your opinion to keep movin', but I'm plumb tuckered out. Bein' over two score and ten years old, an' what with the homeplace bein' torched, uprootin' the family an' all, I'm stoppin' right here in...Tulsa."

Much to everyone's relief, after growling a few unintelligible words and spitting tobacco juice on the ground, a brief prayer was offered by Brother Sin-Eater pleading a safe journey for all concerned. The five Trulucks and Mister Swede gave a hearty goodbye with a teary farewell to those who kept rolling Westward. Since the day we left Missouri, Mama had been called-on dozens of times to care for the sick and feed the hungry. The poor woman was plum worn thin like Daddy. But now, with only her own family to care for, I thought I heard her breathe a sigh of relief. As for the reason of Mister Swede's sudden revelation, I never asked. I was more than ready to get out of that hay wagon and stand upright, again.

****

It was early afternoon when we stopped on the banks of a small bubbling spring to fill the water jugs. When we were all back in the wagon, Daddy followed the meandering creek until we came to another sign planted on the side of the road.

"Tulsa, Ok-la-ho-ma. In-in-ca...cop-orated...?"

"Incorporated," Mister Swede corrected.

"Right," I said and pronounced the word correctly. "Incorporated eighteen-ninety-eight. Edward Calkins, Mayor."

I knew the word "incorporated" meant "joined together" and assumed that Negros, Indians, and whites had ruled out segregation and made Tulsa into an integrated town. Daddy, silent and sober, kept the wagon moving South. I sat up straighter looking for more signs to read, when further ahead a man standing by the side of the road was waving an arm in the air.

"I think he wants us to stop," Mama whispered.

"What do you think, Rose?" Daddy asked out of the corner of his mouth. "Should we, or shouldn't we?"

"I don't think a one-armed man could do us much harm."

"He could be a gun-totin' robber," I added.

"Uh-huh," Daddy grunted. "An' there's no tellin' how many other two-armed bandits are hunkered-down in those bushes."

As we continued to move closer the man removed his black-billed cap and bowed from the waist. When he raised up and smiled ear to ear, it became immediately apparent that besides having only one arm, one of his ears was missing, too.

"Howdy, folks," he said, smacking his lips and grinning wider than a bald-headed jackass with a mouth full of cockleburs.

Daddy looked down at the odd fellow. "Howdy, yourself, mister."

"Might you folks be headin' south?"

"Looks that way," Daddy said.

"Well, if I was yous', I wouldn't cross over them railroad tracks way off yonder."

Everybody in the wagon, including Miss Linnie, rose to their feet. Like a bunch of curious chimpanzees, we all stood, straining our eyes in the direction the old geezer was pointing.

"What's beyond the tracks?" Daddy asked.

"White folk. That there is the Frisco railroad tracks. Owned and operated by Mister Frisco, his-self. If you're a hankerin' to settle in this neck of the woods, you got to carry yourself to Little Africa."

"Is that close by?" Mama asked.

The old man spread his arms wide. "It's all you can see but only north of the Frisco tracks."

Mama, ever the one to get to the bottom of things, asked, "And you, sir? You are out here on your own, to warn others of the immediate dangers ahead?"

The man looked at Mama and hat in hand, bowed his head, again. "I'm here, Madam, by the direct commission of Mister J. B. Stradford, a man of integrity whose only goal is to build a successful Negro community. Upon your consent, I will personally direct you to Mister Stradford, hisself."

After Daddy and Mama held a brief quiet confab, Daddy turned the oxen in the direction the man indicated. I tried to contain my excitement, but the prospect of the Trulucks settling in a place with a name like Little Africa, made me dance a little jig, right there in the wagon where everyone could see my bare skinny legs.

CHAPTER EIGHT
HOME SWEET HOME

Before leaving Missouri, I remember seeing a newspaper photograph of Cornelius Vanderbilt. He was a mutton-chop millionaire who posed for the picture dressed in a Naval uniform topped with golden epaulets. I guess that's why old Corny was referred to as "The Commodore". With whiskers stretching down his cheeks and into a mustache, Mister J. B. Stradford was the spitting image of The Commodore, except that our Mister Stradford wore starched white shirt, black wool jacket, and dark trousers, held up by wide gray suspenders. When he shook hands forcefully with Daddy, Mister Stradford's wire-rim glasses, slid all the way down to hang on the tip of his nose.

While the two men shared a 'plug' of Red Man Chewing Tobacco, Mister Stradford got right friendly. "Just call me J. B., Mister Truluck."

"We-ll, if we're gonna' be on a first name bases, then I'm Simon." Daddy's usual lopsided grin, on his otherwise rugged stoic face, spread from ear to ear.

"Tell me, Simon, what brings you and your family to these parts?"

"We're lookin' to start over, J. B."

"Then you've come to the right place. I'm a bit of a newcomer, myself. Been here since January of this year to be exact." J. B. made sure to look at each one of us, then settled his eyes on Daddy.

"Simon, it's my belief that Negros have a better chance for economic progress if we pool our resources. But be warned, colored people are not welcome south of the Frisco railroad tracks, unless it's to shine a white man's shoes or scrub his wife's dirty floors. The entire city of Tulsa is segregated. As a Negro, you cannot patronize their stores or open one yourself within the city limits." J. B. hooked his thumbs on to the lapels of his jacket and puffed out his chest. "I'm in the process of creating a whole new metropolis, one where Negros can work, play and enjoy the benefits of this wonderful country, without fear of reprisal. I've already purchased several tracts of real estate. I'm in the process of subdividing and selling to Negros only."

"No whites should apply?" Mama blurted out, obviously amazed to hear something so far out of the realm of possibility.

"Now you're talkin' my kind of language," Miss Linnie added.

J. B. gave Mama and Miss Linnie a broad smile. "That's right, ladies. Whites might be welcomed to our side of town to trade, but for damn sure they can't own property or a business." Mister Stratford removed his hat and bowed toward Mama. "You'll please excuse my French, Missus Truluck. As for myself, I intend to build one of the finest hotels West of the Mississippi, right here in Little Africa."

****

We followed behind Mister Stratford's black-fringed surrey for three or four miles, until he reined-in the horses next to a weed-filled parcel of land devoid of trees that was fronted by a dirt road. Still seated in his expensive-looking conveyance, the well-dressed real estate salesman turned to face the ragtag Negro family from Missouri, that now included a white man. If Mister Stratford had an opinion concerning Mister Swede's presence, J. B. kindly kept it to himself.

With a wide sweep of his arm, J. B. announced, "Here it is, folks. One acre of prime real estate in Little Africa."

"Ain't much to see," Miss Linnie grumbled under her breath, then spit a stream of tobacco juice over the sideboards of the wagon.

"The plot is level," Daddy said. "It'll be easy to build on."

It was Mama who asked, "How much?"

J. B. cleared his throat and turned his jowly whiskery jaws up into a big grin. "Since you folks have come on the occasion of my forty-third birthday, I'll let you have this first-rate piece of property for the ridiculously low sum of twenty-five dollars."

When it came to important family decisions, Daddy and Mama put their heads together, which they did for a few moments. I kept my fingers and toes crossed that they would agree to Mister Stradford's terms. To be quite frank, although I was young and healthy, I was tuckered out from living in the old, dilapidated hay wagon.

When Mama nodded "yes", Daddy looked at J. B., and said, "We didn't come this far to be squatters, Mister Stradford. We'll give you one ounce of gold for the property. No more, no less."

"Done, Simon," J. B. remarked, with a big toothy smile that only got bigger. He opened a briefcase that was sitting on the seat of the surrey. "The word of a gentleman is as good as his bond, and sometimes better."

"Mister Swiveller," I blurted. "The Old Curiosity Shop."

J. B.'s head jerked up. He looked over at me, and whispered, "Why, that's absolutely correct, young lady." The real estate salesman turned to Daddy. "You've got a very smart girl there, Simon. But, as I was saying, even though you and I are gentlemen to the core, all you and your lovely wife have to do is sign some papers to make everything legal. Then, the one acre is all yours, to do with whatever you want to do. Ha, of course, that's after you produce an ounce of gold."

After Daddy handed over one ounce of the shiny stuff, he and Mama signed the legal documents. "Thank you, Mister and Missus Truluck, you've made the right decision," Mister Stradford said, then took his leave. The five of us sat in the wagon surveying the situation and dreaming of the future, until my thoughts went to addition and subtraction.

"Daddy, how many dollars for an ounce of gold?"

"Twenty."

"Then we saved five dollars on the deal, right?"

Daddy smiled and nodded. I did too, happy to trade 41 acres for 1 we could call home.

****

As the crow flies, our property was located about a mile north of the Frisco railroad tracks. That geographical location made Mama happy because she wanted to live as far away from white Tulsa as possible. Once everything was unloaded from the wagon, it became a race against time and Mother Nature. The grass was already turning brown, and the once green leaves were taking on a golden tint. Nights had turned chilly, and on some mornings, there was a light frost covering the ground. Indian Summer had definitely arrived.

Jerome and I were assigned to scrounge-up discarded bricks and lumber, while Daddy and Mister Swede dismantled the wagon, board by board. As the work progressed, Mama said it was a tad blasphemous when Mister Swede praised Daddy, saying that he was so a talented with a hammer and nails, he might be related to another carpenter chap who lived two-thousand-years ago.

Once our well was dug and the outhouse erected, I went searching for a lilac bush. As luck would have it, I found a small one growing in an open field. I dug up the roots of a shoot, then planted it in a hole I'd dug next to the outhouse. After pouring water on the loose dirt, I stepped back, gave the lilac twig a hard stare, and whispered, "Now grow, dang it."

****

The first day of 1900 started out cool and sunny but ended on a freezing note. Over the course of a few weeks, Miss Linnie came down with the one-hundred-day croupe. To make matter's worse, she went on and on about her rheu-ma-tiz. Jerome entertained her with his flute, while my job was to apply liberal amounts of Sequah's Oil and Prairie Flower on Miss Linnie's elbows, shoulders and knees every morning and every night. Billed "Sure to cure as the summer sun melts ice", the smelly goop did help relieve the throbbing ache but did nothing for Miss Linnie's grouchy attitude and constant complaining.

The frail woman kept hacking all through January and February. She finally coughed herself to death in early March. We laid her low in a pine box that Daddy had built for the occasion. To feed the attendees at Miss Linnie's wake, our new neighbors supplied baked ham, pinto beans, collard greens and cornbread. Mama commented that with every storm cloud a family suffers through, there's always a silver lining in the distance. I suppose she was right because after Miss Linnie's funeral, Daddy found work as a real carpenter, building coffins for Mister William Callaway's Funeral Home.

****

It soon came to be known within our tight-knit community that if one wanted their loved-one interred inside a seamless coffin guaranteed by Mister Callaway "Not to leak for one-hundred years", then that wooden box had to be built by the one and only Simon Truluck. As far as the one-hundred year "No leak" guarantee, Mister Callaway asserted that by then, Jesus Christ will have returned to Earth, riding in a golden chariot. Therefore water-proof protection provided by the coffin's dove-tailed walnut boards would no longer be needed, since all the deceased would have risen from the dead.

Throughout that spring and summer, Mama's free-range chickens and her green thumb kept us supplied with the bare essentials. We always had a plentiful supply of cornmeal, flour, coffee, sugar, and lard. Commenting about the reproductive cycle of fowl, Mama said, "It's better to have a hen tomorrow than an egg today." To bring in a second income, Daddy built Mama a produce stand on our property facing the street that looked like an oversized chicken coop. Mama was so proud of her new enterprise she nailed a sign on the front of the store that read Rose's Grocery. "Fresh Eggs and Today's Produce" was Mama's main come-on, although when our shelves at home became overstocked, she offered her canned pickled beets, cream-corn and canned green beans, all at reasonable prices.

In exchange for his room and board, Mister Swede continued as a tutor for me and Jerome. I'd learned enough Latin to carry on a conversation and was in the process of learning how to speak Italian. One day, while in our small two-room home with a sleeping porch and a kitchen tacked on in back that served as a schoolroom, I raised my hand to speak.

"Yes," Mister Swede said, his voice exhibiting a touch of impatience, probably due to the fact that I'd been chattering all day. "What is it, now, Olivia?"

When I rose to my feet to speak, I asked, "Why am I learning Italian? It's almost the same as Latin. Why not let me try another language?"

Mister Swede pointed to his nose and said, "Olivia, look at this parish pickax. Do you know why it's so long and sharp?" I shook my head. "It's because I can sniff out real talent. You my dear, have the unique ability to learn Chinese, Swahili or even Appalachian Mountain slang. The reason why learning Italian is so important, is because it's the language of poets."

I thought about what Mister Swede had just told me, then

53

asked, "Mister Swede, don't you write poetry?" He silently nodded. "You must be good at thinking up things, right?" He nodded again. "Then tell me, why do white people hate Negros?"

"Prejudice, bigotry, jealously. I could go on and on, Olivia, but…"

"I guess what I meant to ask, what makes you so sympathetic to Negros? You're not one, or are you?" I probably should have stopped there but instead, I kept rambling. "Sometimes, if the mother is light skinned and the father is white, their child might come out whiter than white."

Mister Swede shook his head, and said, "No".

"But you're not like the other white people – the ones who hate us."

Mister Swede smiled and nodded. "I lay all my liberal notions directly on the doorstep of my mother, Louise Ann Greeley. She taught me to scrutinize the character of an individual, not judge the person by the color of their skin." Mister Swede pointed to his cheek where one tiny black speck of tar had stuck so tight it might never be removed except surgically. With a flourish of his hand, my tutor, said, "I'm keeping that spot as a black badge of honor. You see, Olivia, I come from a long line of American Abolitionists who believe that all men and women are created equal."

"It's just so sad," I whispered.

"What is?" Mister Swede asked.

"Even after so many colored folks and white men were killed during the war for emancipation…Negros are still segregated from the rest of white society?"

"I'm afraid it would take a miracle from heaven to end the blatant racism that has been with this country since its beginning."

"Well, I'll tell you one thing, Mister Swede. I'll never ever step one toe south of the Frisco railroad tracks. For all I care, those white people can have Tulsa, I'm happy staying right here in Little Africa.".

CHAPTER NINE
W-O-M-A-N

By 1905, the year I turned fifteen, Little Africa had been renamed the Greenwood District. Every Saturday morning, white girls from Tulsa, bodaciously gussied-up in frills and lace, would parade along Greenwood Avenue, acting like princesses in horseless carriages. The posers wore big wide hats with ostrich feathers that stuck out high in the air, ruffled white satin blouses and belts thin as rubber-bands wrapped around teeny, tiny waists held up long black skirts. I tended to run around in a pair of men's trousers if I could find any to fit and a collarless white shirt, or pantaloons with a peasant blouse. I suppose I tended to dress more like a man, not because I wanted to be one, but to be treated as an equal.

I kept my opinion concerning women's fashion to myself. As far as I was concerned, it was supposed to be a free country, so people should be allowed to drape their bodies with whatever suited their fancy. But, no matter what sort of outfit they wore, I still had a hard time telling one white person from another. To me, Whitey looked – unfinished – like God forgot to give them color.

My latte-colored skin had darkened with age to a light-bronze color. My almond-shaped eyes and high cheek bones led me to suspect there might be a Red Man hiding in the family woodshed. Finally, after much prodding, Daddy admitted that my grandma's first name was Schon. He said it was from the Lakota and means 'beautiful one'. But according to Mama, "Beauty is only skin deep."

I was smart enough to know that a woman, especially one who's a Negro, needs a brain to go along with the hourglass figure.

It was one balmy afternoon, while helping Mama in her produce stand, that I asked, "Mama, why is it that sometimes I get so fidgety? I used to be able to sit still and read for hours. Now, after a few minutes, my mind starts to wander, and I can't concentrate on even one word."

Mama took a bite off a juicy red apple, chewed a few times, then thoughtfully said, "That's 'cause jus' like you, Mother Nature's got cycles. From top to bottom on the outside, you've changed. Same goes for what's inside, too." Mama eyeballed the apple ready to take another bite but lowered it. "You see, Olivia, a lady's insides are different than a man. Especially her plumbing." Mama gave me a big smile. "Remember when your breasts started growin'? Remember how sore and tender they were?"

"Yeah...they hurt for a long time. That's when I started wearing those tight slips. I hated those things."

"Now that you're a filled-out woman, you need more support, a lot more." Mama nodded at my breasts. "Up there."

"I made a sour face then jutted out my chest. "Because of these two boobies, I can't participate in Mister Swede's archery classes anymore. Not unless I went all Amazon and cut off the right one. And if it's okay with you, I'd just as soon go without the baling wire and steel hooks."

Mama grunted, shook her head and clicked her tongue. "Olivia, it ain't proper for a lady to give her breasts free range. Somethin' about seein' those things bouncin' around makes men get funny ideas an' go whole hog on a woman."

"Oh, my, Mama," I said rolling my eyes, then putting a hand to my cheek in mock surprise. "I sure wouldn't want to be responsible for making a man hot under the collar or anywhere else. He might do something we'd surely regret."

****

Hogs are defined as being piggish when it comes to food they eat, and they live in total squalor. Even though the image of a boy going 'whole hog' on my body made me want to vomit, it didn't deter me from trying to find out what all the hubbub was about when it came to courting. Being under the private tutelage of Mister Swede made meeting boys somewhat difficult. But as a member of the Ebenezer Baptist Church Choir, Sunday mornings put me in close proximity with the opposite sex.

A person would be wrong if they thought I only attended church to meet boys. I admit that was one of the reasons, but not the only one, there were two more. One was Mama. She always wore her biggest frown when I balked at sitting through one of Brother Sin-Eaters loud long-winded sermons. Now, the pastor of the Ebenezer Baptist Church, a younger and much more soft-spoken man than Brother Sin-Eater, went on for hours, preaching the same brand of Old Time Religion. But I sat and listened because it made Mama smile.

Finally, I just liked to sing, and that's why on Sunday morning, I was standing next to Mister Tall Dark and Handsome, Jesse Jefferson. The boy with wavy black hair and lively brown eyes, was two years my senior, but when he hit a high note, I swear the church steeple shook, the bell rung, the floor vibrated and for a split second my heart stopped beating.

It was the day of the First Ebenezer Baptist Church's Women's Box-Lunch Auction. I entered an assortment of hard-boiled eggs, crackers and pickled pig's feet all nestled inside an old Easter basket. I was sure his tongue was planted firmly in his cheek when Mister Swede said, "Any man would be lucky to have the winning bid for that tantalizing array of edibles."

When my box-lunch came up for auction, I held my breath and closed my eyes, hoping someone would have the guts to make a bid. The church pastor started the bidding at one dollar. When there were no takers, he lowered the price to fifty cents. In the ensuing deafening silence, I forced back tears that were threatening to well-up in my eyes and contemplated making a dash for the exit. How much embarrassment could a girl endure?

Then I heard someone yell, "Two dollars."

"Going once, going twice, sold." Those words were such sweet music to my red, burning ears.

An hour later, when the two of us were sitting on a quilt under the shade of an old oak tree, dining on the contents of my box-lunch, Jesse bent over to whisper, "To the lovely lady Olivia, whom I admire without trivia."

I laughed at his doggerel. "I might forgive you for being flippant about Coleridge, but I don't think Dorothy Wordsworth would think it a bit funny."

Jesse and I hit it off right away. Over the next few days, we recited poetry to each other and discussed the latest novel we had read. Kissing amounted to a quick peck on the cheek. I spent nights alone in bed, staring up at the ceiling, asking the same question over and over.

"What do I want in a man, an intellectual companion, a trusted friend or a passionate lover? The answer always came back, why not all three?"

****

In the spring of 1905, after the April showers, Mother Nature went totally berserk. She unleashed a rip-snortin' tornado that touched down in the far southwestern part of the Oklahoma Territory, then took a northeasterly direction. Two and one-half hours later the powerful twister had sent over 112 people to Kingdom Come and wiped-out Snyder, Oklahoma. Nineteen-oh-five was also the year of the first Oklahoma oil boom and the year Daddy quit making coffins to work in the oil fields.

Our new cozy two-bedroom home had a parlor, living room, slanted tin roof, double entry and wide front porch. It might have looked rustic, but it kept us warm and dry. It was one evening in the kitchen after a bountiful dinner of fried chicken, boiled cabbage and sweet potato pie. I was helping Mama clear dinner dishes from the table. Daddy leaned back in his chair and stuffed his favorite corncob pipe full of sweet-smelling pipe tobacco. Once the white smoke was swirling above his head, Daddy sat up straighter to let out a satisfying burp.

"Daddy," I said, careful not spill the coffee I was pouring into his cup, "Mama says passing gas and belching at the table is very impolite."

"Uh-huh," he grunted, puffing away on his pipe. "Now, now, Missy, don't go havin' one of your conniption fits over a natural bodily function.

With sweet potato pie on his face, Jerome put in his two cents. "You know, Pa. Olivia is gettin all uppity an' big in the britches. It's 'cause she's in love with Jesse Jefferson."

I placed the blue enamel coffee pot on the table and gave my brother the meanest look I could muster. "Why don't you mind your own business, Jer-ome."

"Now, now, you two," Daddy said, trying to make his scratchy voice sound ominous.

"Daddy," I asked, "can you get Jesse a job on the oil rigs?"

"Tell you what, Stringbean, I…"

"Daddy."

"Oh yeah, that's right, I ain't supposed to call you that name no more."

"She prefers to be called O-li-vi-a," Jerome said, his voice so sickeningly sweet it made me want to gag.

"That's right," I said, looking directly at Daddy. "And from now on, I'm going to call you Father. Daddy sounds so…so infantile."

Mama, who had just come into the kitchen, brushed the top of my head with her hand. "Our little girl's getting' all growed-up, Simon."

Father looked at me and smiled. "You tell your beau to come down to Sue Bland Number one. He can start out on the oil rig as a gofer an' work up to floorhand."

"Sue Bland Number One," Jerome said. "That was one big gusher, right, Pa?"

Father nodded in agreement and turned to look at me. "Your Jesse can get on, just as long as he get's along with the Irish cracker boss man."

"Simon," Mama said, eyeballing Father probably over his use of the word cracker.

"If there's any slip-up on the rig," Father continued, "it's always the 'Nigger's fault'. I dunno' but maybe that potato famine addled his brain."

"Eating green potatoes is like eating poison," I said, remembering that bit of information from something I'd read.

"If the boss at the oil riggin' job's so bad, why don't you quit, Pa?" Jerome persisted. "You could go back to making coffins."

"Because sonny-boy, the pay for a roughneck is four times what a coffin carpenter makes."

Mister Swede, who was sitting off to the side, rattled the newspaper he'd been reading and pointed at the headline. "It says here that Mister Booker T. Washington will visit our Greenwood community in the coming months. He will be the keynote speaker at an event sponsored by the Negro Chamber of Commerce." Mister Swede methodically folded the newspaper, placed it on the table and nodded at Daddy. "Mister Truluck, in the furtherance of their complete education, I recommend that Olivia and Jerome attend this speech given by Mister Washington. The price of attendance is a pittance compared to the amount of knowledge they'll acquire."

"Mister Swede," Father said. "With your silver tongue you could sell long-handles to the Australian aborigines."

Mister Swede gave Daddy a curt bow of his head. "Thank you for that ambiguous compliment, Mister Truluck. But I'm an educator and as such my 'Normal School for Boys and Girls, ages eight through sixteen' is and always has been my one true passion. Education is the only hope for the Negro race. It's time to throw off the shackles of segregation by teaching the young how to think for themselves. There's hope for humanity if we all do the right thing."

"Is that so?" Father replied and looked across the table to catch Mama's eye. She nodded, and after clearing his throat, Father continued. "Mister Swede, Rose and I have decided to parlay a portion of our savings into your all Negro school."

Mister Swede's mouth dropped wide open. When the words finally came, he gushed, "Thank you, Mister...and Missus Truluck, not only for your generosity but for putting your faith and trust in me. I'm honored to have won your confidence. Now, with your financial help, my dream can be a reality. I've found a small space to rent on Greenwood Avenue. Once I can get my school chartered, then I can open it to the public. Negro children, no matter what their economic status, will be welcome."

I thought about the consequences of graduating from an accredited public school, and asked, "Does that mean next year, I'll get a real sheepskin?"

"Yes, Olivia," Mister Swede said.

Mama came over and patted Mister Swede's shoulder. "And of course, Olivia and Jerome will attend Mister Washington's oration. But there's only one problem."

I looked up and asked, "What's that, Mama?"

"Well, my Dear, if you're going out in public, you want to look your best."

"That's right, O-li-vi-a," Jerome blathered. "Maybe Mister Jesse Jefferson will be there."

I ignored my brother's ingratiating comment and looked at Mama. "I'm not sure if I have anything to look my best in."

****

As it turned out, the following Wednesday evening, during a

break in choir practice, when I stepped outside for a breath of fresh air, I spied a female choir member in the arms of Mister Jesse Jefferson. Needless to say, I not only quit the choir, but much to Mama's dislike, I quit the Ebenezer Baptist Church as well.

CHAPTER TEN
CUTTING CONTEST

As the Greenwood District grew in size so did Mama's grocery business. There was more than one occasion when customer demand outstripped her supply of yard eggs and fresh produce. Father had more than doubled the size of the truck garden but when tomatoes or corn were out of season, or an army of caterpillars attacked the collard greens, Mama had to search high and low to find worthy produce. To help supplement the family's income, Mister Swede suggested that I browse the Daily Greenwood Newspaper's help-wanted ads.

It was one bright morning, and I was sitting at the kitchen table reading the want ads out loud so that Mama could hear. "Wanted. Translator. Call Central 701'. Mmmmm, the ad doesn't say what languages need translated. I can speak Latin, Italian and some French. Then again maybe the job is for white's only. Mama, do you think I should call?"

Mama placed a pair of Father's work trousers she was mending on the table. When she looked at me, there was such love in her eyes and concern in her voice that it made me want to cry. Mama reached out to hold my chin up with her thumb and forefinger.

"Olivia, how many times have I told you that to succeed in life all it takes is determination. Remember Dear, a woman without inner-fortitude, no matter if she's Colored or white, lives on her knees."

"All right then," I said, sitting up a little straighter. "I'll call. But later. Maybe tomorrow."

"Don't put off what you--"

"Mama," I interrupted, "I'll call tomorrow, just not now, okay?"

"And remember, Olivia," she scolded, "when you apply for a job in person, a sincere smile is worth a thousand words in any language." Mama then switched conversational gears, and asked, "Olivia, have you given any thought about what you're going to wear when Mister Booker T. Washington comes to town?"

"That's all I've been thinking about. I don't want anything bulky or fussy and I hate ruffles and bows. They make a girl look like...like a Joplin prosti-"

"Olivia," Mama grunted. "I'll not have that kind of talk in my house. I take it you want to dress in practical clothes. No ribbon for you, is that it?" Mama sorted through a stack of material laying on her sewing table until she found a swath of black wool. She held it up for my inspection.

"This will do for a suit jacket," she said. "We'll add shoulder pads and tailor it to fit like a glove. Some flat silk braid here and there, and maybe a tiny bit of embroidery to the bodice to butter up the bacon. Now stand up and I'll take your measurements."

While Mama was measuring the length of my arm, from the shoulder to the wrist, I asked, "Mama, instead of a skirt to go with this jacket, can you make trousers with hip pockets?"

Mama stopped her measuring. She tilted her head and gave me the strangest look. "Olivia, why would you want to wear something like that?"

"Well, for one thing, pants are more comfortable when you're getting on and off a horse or climbing on a wagon. Secondly, I'm tired of tripping over my own skirt, especially when I walk up steps. I've got to lift it up or fall flat on my face. Thirdly trousers don't raise up in a wind. If I want to be accepted as an equal to men, it won't hurt to dress like one, now will it, Mama?"

She had to stop and think about my question for a minute until finally, Mama said, "No, Dear, it won't hurt at all. Now, if you want to wear long pants, step up on this stool and let me measure your inseam. Then, I'll show you how to cut and sew trousers."

"But I already know how to thread a needle."

"Not for trousers, Dear. Now, stand up straight to your full height." Mama let out a grunt while getting down on her knees. Holding one end of the measuring tape at the V where my inner leg met my crotch, she looked up. There was a look of amazement in her eyes. "Good Lord, Child, how tall are you?"

"Tall enough to be noticed," I said, thinking about how all the men and boys' eyes followed me when I sashayed along Greenwood Avenue.

When she was finished with pinning and marking with chalk, Mama slowly got to her feet with the help of a few grunts and gave me another thorough once-over. "My, my," she wheezed, shaking her head. "You're all grown up. How did you do it so fast?"

"I dunno'. It just happened."

"You're a woman now. You know what that means, don't you?"

I stepped of the stool and shrugged. "No, Mama. What does it mean?"

Mama laid her tape measure on the table. The solemn tone in her voice held a warning. "It don't matter if the heifer's black as coal or lumpy as a mattress, if a bull's hungry enough, he'll do most anything to taste those vittles." Mama looked me in the eye and pointed her forefinger at my chest. "All you gotta' do is figure out which man is worthy enough. An' Olivia. While you're looking for the right man, remember that a merry companion makes for pleasant music on the journey."

"Yes, Mama."

****

I swear, Mister Booker T. Washington's face was plastered on every telephone pole, store window and billboard in the Greenwood District. With all the manic hoopla, one would have thought that the president of the United States was coming to our all-Negro town. Today was the big day. Mister Swede, Jerome and I walked along the street enjoying the red, white and blue banners flapping in the wind. We were headed in the direction of the city park where Mister Washington was scheduled to give his speech.

Jerome pointed at the huge three-story brick building in the distance. The brash excitement in his voice was contagious. "That's where he's staying."

"Ah, yes," Mister Swede said. "The J. B. Stradford Hotel."

"The most luxurious hotel in the Oklahoma Territory," I added.

As we approached the Dimebox Theatre, Jerome pointed again, only this time he tugged on Mister Swede's sleeve with his free hand.

"Mister Swede, Mister Swede. Look, what's playing at the Dimebox."

"The Little Train Robbery," I said. "A sequel to The Great Train Robbery. With an all-child cast. That's most unusual, I'd say."

"Psssst," Mister Swede hissed. "Parodies are for weak minds. What have I been warning you two about?"

"Stay away from dime movies and penny candy," Jerome and I replied in a sequenced syncopated rhythm.

Two blocks further on we came to a garishly painted juke joint, sandwiched between a cigar store and a billiard parlor. Mister Swede stopped and turned to address Jerome.

"All the big bugs play here, Jerome," Mister Swede said, and pointed to the ramshackle building. A sign hanging over the door read "Blue Front". Jerome silently nodded. Mister Swede bent over to get eye-to-eye with my brother. "You can do it, Jerome. You can keep up with the best of them. You're a bricky boy, right?"

Jerome had kept a tight grip on the black case he was carrying. He whispered, "I guess so."

"Guess so?" Mister Swede hissed.

"Know so," Jerome shot back.

Ah, my younger brother. What can be said about a thirteen-year-old musical genius whose britches were too small for his big rear end. He had a handsome, open face which made him a hit for girls. But today, he was jittery as a polecat. Although, he'd been playing the clarinet since he was nine, Jerome had never performed in front of a crowd. The whites of his brown eyes were as big as butter plates when he swore, "I can do it, Mister Swede. I know it."

"Excellent." Mister Swede pulled a pocket watch from inside his vest and checked the time. "We have over an hour before Mister Washington speaks. C'mon, Jerome let's go show 'em what you've got."

Inside the Blue Front, it was standing room only. With

Mister Swede in the lead, the three of us managed to worm our way through the laughing, dancing crowd, until we came to where a six-man band was launching a fierce attack of syncopated rhythm. I swear, they made the whole shack shake, shimmy, and shudder, including Two Ton Tessie quaking in the corner.

Mister Swede tapped his toe on the floor and shouted over the din, "The only way you can sit still listening to Ragtime, is if you're already dead."

After the six-man band finished The Ticklish Rag, Mister Swede approached the bandstand. After a few words with the band leader, our tutor motioned for Jerome to come on stage.

A hush fell over the crowd when the M. C. announced, "Ladies and gentlemen – it looks like we're in for some fun. Mister Jerome Truluck, the young man standing next to me, challenges all clarinet players to a cutting contest, one at a time or all in one stick."

Jerome opened the black case. After inserting a new reed into his clarinet, the fledging professional musician, put the musical instrument to his lips then broke into a four/four version of the piano scales. With a confident nod of his head, Jerome indicated he was ready for all comers.

He met and bested every challenger. Jerome's chord progressions of rhythmic harmony caused the crowd to stomp their feet and clap their hands. When the cutting contest had given up its last man, Jerome stood alone on the stage.

"You took the egg," Mister Swede yelled, his usually white cheeks had become a cheery cherry-red color.

My Brother didn't have long to bask in the admiration, Mister Swede quickly hustled us out of the Blue Front. By the time we arrived at the city park, the area in front of the speaker's platform was packed with people. There seemed to be a high voltage charge in the atmosphere, like we were all plugged into the same receptacle, causing the hair on the back of my neck to stand up.

CHAPTER ELEVEN
DREAM LOVER

If the festive crowd's lively chatter, their boisterous laughing and incessant 'wolf whistles' wasn't exhilarating enough, a man on the bandstand put a megaphone up to his mouth. "Ladies and gentlemen, may I have your attention, please. Today, it gives me great pleasure to introduce a giant of a man. A man who, during the lynching of Negros in the mid-nineties, gave us hope with his Atlanta compromise. Today, in the Territory of Oklahoma, that hope for Negro equality is becoming a reality. So, without further-adieu, I give you the Honorable Booker T. Washington."

After a monstrous round of huzzahs and what seemed like more than five minutes of non-stop clapping, Booker T. Washington took the stage. He was a big man all right, with short-cropped hair and an intelligent-looking face. When he spoke, his words came across in a thundering voice. Unlike most, the Honorable Mister Washington didn't need a megaphone to get his point across.

"I'm a peace-loving man," he boomed. "You should be, too. We gain nothing by using the tactic of violence. Burning. Looting. That only makes the white man hate us more. What we need is intelligent cooperation between one another. I'm here today to tell you how to help one another in your own community. We did in Tuskegee, Alabama, and so can you."

As Mister Washington went on speechifying, I happened to innocently glance to my right. Girls aren't supposed to stare so I quickly looked away. Then, every time I sneaked a peek, he'd catch me. I must say, there was an immediate attraction when my brown eyes landed on his green ones. We held each other's undivided attention, until Mister Washington bellowing snapped my mind back to the present situation.

"We as Colored people will not be disenfranchised from the American dream. We will go our own way and not be drug into the cesspool of bigotry and prejudice that plagues this wonderful country."

The crowd gave up an enthusiastic round of applause and roars of approval. When the celebrated speaker descended from the stage, he shook hands with the men and tipped his hat to the ladies. Jerome tugged on Mister Swede's arm and pointed to the group of musicians who were setting instruments up on the bandstand."

"Mister Swede, can I?"

Our tutor nodded his approval. Several men came over and started chatting with Mister Swede. I searched the crowd for the green-eyed man, but he had disappeared. Then, a bald-headed man joined the group and in a loud Brother Sin-Eater voice, introduced himself as Mister Edwin McCabe, the auditor for the state of Kansas.

With one hand raised like he was taking the oath of office, McCabe swore, "By God, I say we coordinate an appeal directly to the U. S. Government to make Oklahoma an all-Negro state."

"What about the Indians and the white men?" Mister Swede asked. "Why, if you try total segregation there will be head-splitting trafficking in the streets."

"I have no doubt there will be rowdy behavior," McCabe stated, using his forefinger as a pointer to heaven.

"Negros will declare eminent domain and buy out any of those who might object. Otherwise, they'll have to voluntarily deed their property over to the new state of Afrikana."

"And the mineral rights?" Mister Swede added.

"All Afrikanars will share equally in the oil royalties."

Mister Swede shook his head. "That sounds like blatant discrimination, maybe even Socialism, if not cause for armed revolution."

Mister McCabe put a forefinger and thumb to his chin and hummed, "It could be, it could be."

Another man stepped up and said, "I say we all move back to Africa. Our forefathers are from that land, cut the roots and the tree dies."

"Rep-er-a-tions," a third man said, dragging out the word. "Forty acres and a mule? To hell with that. For ten years I lived a slave. I deserve a hundred acres and a pension from Uncle Sam for the harsh treatment I endured. And I've got the scars to prove it."

It was at that moment the green-eyed man appeared. Now, he was looking directly at me and walking in my direction. I tried not to panic and kept my feet firmly planted. He took his time coming over, shaking hands along the way, why he even stopped to sign his autograph for a young lady. When he finally came near enough, he looked in my eyes, bowed, then smiled mischievously. That's when I realized his eyes weren't exactly green, but a dark shade of cyan.

"Madam," he said, with a voice almost as deep as Mister Washington's. "You are a rare gem that outshines any diamond." He bowed again then asked, "May I be so bold as to introduce myself?" All I could do was silently stare and nod. "The name is Bingham, James Bingham, and I'm more than pleased to seek the company of Miss...?"

From the brim of his black derby with his dark curly hair peeking out from underneath, all the way down to his white spats and highly polished black shoes, James Bingham was a model of perfection. He had a straight even jaw with a cleft in his chin. Tall and graceful, he spoke good English and his smile was so sincere it made me shiver. Manners say a lady should never willingly give her age but says nothing about giving her name.

"Truluck," I finally said. "Miss Olivia Truluck."

"A beautiful name for a fine-looking woman." He tipped his derby with one hand and held out the other one. When I placed my hand in his, he quickly brought it up to his lips. My heart started beating faster and my stomach clenched. I could feel the male heat emanating from his physical presence and wanted to feel his strong arms wrapped around my body.

"I take it you're here to support Mister Washington?" James asked.

"Yes."

"I'm fond of the Greenwood District. An all-Negro community is a wonderful idea. As a matter of fact, I'm thinking one day I may settle here."

"Why not now?" I asked, wondering if I was sounding too imprudent, especially since Mister Bingham and I had just met.

"Because, Miss Truluck, I'm a travelin' man."

"Oh?"

He laughed and shook his head vigorously. "I play in the Negro Baseball League." He pointed to his head. "It's a fact, you've got to be a little crazy up here to be a ball player."

James and I talked on and on about baseball and a million other things, until the band stopped playing. He had a way of looking deep into my eyes that not only melted my heart and gave me goose bumps but left me breathless to boot.

"May I have the pleasure of walking you home, Miss Truluck," he asked.

"I...I came with my tutor and brother. And please, Mister Bingham, call me Olivia."

He nodded and gave me another one of his sincere toothy smiles. "Okay, Olivia. Shall we find your escorts?"

"Why, thank you Mister Bingham."

"It's James."

I smiled and nodded. "I should go round up those two myself."

"Do I have permission to call on you?" he asked, rotating his derby hat around and around with both hands.

"Of course," I said, thinking that if James didn't call me, I'd would find out how to call on him.

He committed my telephone number to memory, and we parted with a handshake. I searched the dwindling crowd for Mister Swede and Jerome, but I came up empty and decided they had probably already left the park. I'd done it before, so I walked home alone that evening, wondering if the knot in my stomach was due to the fact that I was mad at Mister Swede and my brother for ditching me, or because I'd fallen head over heels for a baseball player.

****

Once I arrived home, hoping not to wake the folks, I slid open my bedroom window and quietly climbed inside. After disrobing, I laid flat on my back in my bed, in the dark, staring at the water stains on the ceiling. I conjured up the image of Mister Bingham, wearing that irresistible smile. As I closed my eyes to fall asleep, that good-looking young devil blew me a goodnight kiss. I swear he did!

In my dream that night, I was standing behind home-plate. James Bingham stood opposite me on the pitcher's mound. There was fire in his eyes, as he positioned his left foot on the rubber and went into the wind-up. The white dot streaked across the sixty-foot distance and at the last second, curved off and disappeared into the ether. Then I was incased in James's arms. He pulled me close and whispered, "It's all in the wrist." When he kissed me like I'd never been kissed before, it tasted like sweet butter with cream on top.

****

The next morning, even before the rooster crowed or the sun had a chance to rise for the daily occasion, I heard Mama hollering, "Jerome. Jerome, where in thunder are you? This is your morning to help open Rose's Grocery."

I rolled out of bed, threw on a work shirt, a pair of Father's old trousers then stepped into the hallway. I was surprised to see Mama come rushing out the door toward me, gasped, "Olivia. Where is your brother?"

I shrugged and pointed toward the enclosed back porch, where Jerome usually landed for the night. "Did you check his pallet?"

"Of course, I did, Olivia. That's the first place I looked. He's not anywhere in the house nor did I see him outside. Oh, good Lord. He didn't come home last night, did he?"

"Are you sure, Mama?"

Mama looked at me and she wasn't smiling. "Yes, I am. His pallet hasn't been touched."

Jerome did have slovenly habits such as leaving his clothes where Mama or I had to pick them up and of course he never made-up his bed.

"Last night," I said. "Jerome was playing in the band up on the stage. He did a wonderful job of keeping up the other musicians. I just wonder where he could have gone?"

Worry lines were furrowing into Mama's forehead. "Mister Swede hasn't seen him, either. He thought Jerome had come home with you."

"No, Mama," I said, slowly shaking my head. "I walked home by myself."

"You what? Olivia, what have I told you over and over about walking around after dark? You have to have a…"

"A chaperone," I said. "Yes, yes, I know, I know. But you see, Mama, last night I met someone. He was…very special."

"So special you abandoned your brother, and left him alone?"

"Mama," I gasped. "It was Jerome who left without me."

By that time Father had come in to join the discussion. "What's all the hubbub about?"

"Jerome's missing," Mama huffed and gave me what I

considered to be a mean look.

"I...I thought Jerome was with Mister Swede. You see, I was talking to Mister Bingham, and I..."

"Mister Bingham?" Father interjected. "I've never met a Bingham. Who's this Bingham fellow?"

"He's a baseball player, Father. He plays for the Kanas City Monarchs. As a matter of fact, he invited me to a baseball game tomorrow. I was wanting to know if I could go."

"I don't care if Mister Bingham plays tiddlywinks for the New York Yankees," Mama blurted with her clenched fists on her hips. "What I want to know is what has happened to our Jerome."

"Have you found the lad yet?" Mister Swede asked, shuffling into the room.

"No," Mama said.

Mister Swede tried to fill in the blanks. "It was my bursitis acting up. I could hardly move my left arm, so I left the park while the band was still playing. Jerome was really blowing a lick, he was." Mister Swede turned to look at me. "I was going to tell you, Olivia, but you were in such deep conversation with a man, I didn't want to interrupt."

"You assumed wrong, Mister Swede," Mama said. "Olivia wasn't conversing, she was flirting with that Mister James Bingham." Mama looked at me and shook her head from side to side. "And she didn't have time to worry about her brother."

CHAPTER TWELVE
BANANA JOHN

After a lengthy discussion around the Truluck kitchen table, Father advised that the best plan of action was for us not to panic. Mister Swede suggested that Jerome had probably spent the night with one of the other musicians. To placate Mama's fear that her missing boy was not in serious trouble, Father and Mister Swede agreed to conduct a thorough search of the Greenwood District. When the two men left the house, they headed south toward the Frisco railroad tracks. Mama and I did what we always did and opened Rose's Grocery.

Once everything had settled down in the store, I decided to make the call. I picked up the receiver from the telephone mounted on the wall and turned the crank. There was a buzzing sound then a switchboard operator asked in a scratchy voice, "Number, pul-ease?"

"Central seven-oh-one, please."

Two rings on the other end of the line, a man's voice. "Ciao."

"Hello. I'm calling about the translator job."

"Che cosa?"

I asked, "Lavoro di Traduttore."

"Si?"

"Dove mi candido."

"Tulsa. Quattro e ventidue Seventh Street. Numero otto.

Nove in punto. Va bene."

"Grazie. Fino a domini," I said and hung up the receiver. When I hung up the receiver, I noticed that Mama was in front of the store with a customer. "Good," I thought, "she didn't hear a word."

****

That afternoon while Mama and I were restocking the shelves in the grocery store, the telephone buzzed. She jumped up and made a beeline for the phone. I listened-in on the conversation.

"Hello?" There was a sense of urgent worry in Mama's voice when she asked, "Jerome is where? My God, is he hurt? Yes? No. All right, goodbye."

Mama silently placed the telephone receiver back on wall. Like nothing important had happened, she knelt on the floor then tore open a case of blackstrap molasses.

I couldn't take the deafening silence a second longer. I placed my hands on my hips, looked at Mama, and asked, "Well?"

Mama started putting jars of molasses on the shelf. "Olivia, you should have kept an eye on him."

"I know that now, Mama. But I thought-.

"No, you didn't think. Otherwise, Jerome wouldn't be locked up in jail. "What was more important that you couldn't keep an eye on him?"

I felt the heat start to rise in my neck. When the hot anger had risen to a boiling point, I stomped my foot on the wooden floor so hard it made the molasses jars rattle.

"I told you, Mama. I was talking to Mister James Bingham. I lost track of time and as far as Jerome is concerned, I'm sorry he got in trouble but it's not my fault. I can't be my brother's keeper all the time. Now, can you tell me if he's all right?"

Mama slowly rose to her feet with a grunt and looked straight at me without saying a word. When the bells tinkled above the front door, she turned away.

"We'll talk about this at a later time," Mama said, over her shoulder, and went to help Missus Williams find the perfect head of lettuce.

****

By suppertime, the whole world could breathe easier. Jerome was home with both feet securely anchored under the Truluck's dinner table. Mister Swede was away preparing his school for the grand opening in the fall. It was just the four of us. Mama had prepared a special homecoming meal of pork chops, greasy cream gravy, roasted beets and Jerome's favorite, smashed potatoes smothered in garlic butter. While everyone wolfed down her cooking, I sat toying with my food. I was both glad and angry. Except for the goose egg on his forehead, Jerome had returned home relatively unscathed. But I was still catching the blame.

Mama went to retrieve an apple pie from the windowsill, so I took the opportunity to ask, "Jerome, did you meet any interesting people while you were in the calaboose?"

Jerome mumbled, "No," then stuffed his mouth full of mashed potatoes. Finally, after chugging a glass of milk with an inch of cream floating on top, he belched, and said, "I did see a man get his ear bit off."

"Jerome," Mama said, placing the pie she'd baked on the table. "I will not have that kind of talk in my house."

"Ewwww, that's horrible," I said. "How can any of you eat with a picture like that in your head?"

"Only snitches get stitches, right Jerome?" Father and Jerome had a good laugh, but I didn't find their joking one bit amusing.

Mama looked at Jerome. When she shook her head, I knew he was in for one of her sermons. "I hope you learned a good lesson, boy. Next time somebody tells you the grass is greener on the other side of the tracks don't you believe a word of it. If somebody tol' you to jump off the bridge, would you do it?"

"That's right, Jerome," I said, finally breaking into a grin. "Don't believe nothin' of what you hear. And watch out for high bridges."

"Olivia," Mama barked.

After stuffing their stomachs with the sweet pastry, Father and Jerome went outside to sit on the front porch. I helped Mama clear the dinner table. When we had all the dirty dishes piled up in the sink, she stopped, looked at me then took my hand in hers.

"Olivia, Dear. Now that I've had time to think about it, I understand."

"You do? Mama nodded. "Then you're not mad at me anymore?"

"I was never mad at you. Oh, maybe a little. I was disappointed. You've always looked after Jerome, but now that he's older, that boy's got to learn for himself how to stay out of trouble."

Mama started scraping the dishes clean, then stopped. There was a far-away look was in her eyes when she said, "I remember how I felt the first time I saw your father. It was on a bright Sunday afternoon at a church social. I was wearing my good gingham dress with a matching bonnet. He was dressed in a hand-me-down black suit that didn't fit him in the shoulders. The trousers were high-waters and his jacket sleeves barely came down to his wrists." Lost down memory lane, Mama looked at me and smiled. "I wonder just how much of that day your father remembers?"

"Last night, Mister Bingham told me that I'm a rare gem."

Mama snapped out of her reverie. "Uh-huh," she grunted. "Olivia, what were you teasing Jerome about earlier?"

"Never believe nothing of what you hear."

"That's right, Dear. And now I'm going to tell you something and I want you to believe every word I'm saying. When that Mister Bingham starts whispering sweet nothings in your ear, I want you to remind him that the milk is not free, and that love comes with a hefty price."

"Which is, Mama?"

"Commitment and compromise. Now, enough of this love talk. Your brother is back home, and all is well."

"Tomorrow is my job interview."

"That's wonderful, Dear?"

"I wasn't going to tell you. That way if I didn't get the job you wouldn't be disappointed. You were already upset with me over Jerome."

"Olivia," Mama whispered, touching my cheek with her fingers. "You've never really failed me."

"Well," I said with a sigh, "looks like I'll finally have to cross the dang Frisco railroad tracks."

"Olivia, not in my house, please."

****

It was well before sunrise the next morning when Mister Swede and I hitched Father's white stocking mare to the family's new black surrey. Although it was a Sunday, due to my quest for gainful employment, Mama Rose had excused me from attending church services. Mister Swede and I rode in high style down the street that had recently been named, Greenwood Avenue.

When we came to a one-story red brick building, I pointed at the marquee. "Oh, Mister Swede, look. The Dime box is showing The Black Hand. On the way back home let's catch the matinee."

Mister Swede leaned forward, read the words posted on the marquee, then grunted his disapproval. "Motion picture theaters, they're ten times worse than those perverted dens of inequities commonly called pool halls." Mister Swede clucked his tongue and with the snap of his crop, hurried the bay along while squeezing in the last word. "Moving pictures are for men who wear gas pipes without a belt and women of suspect character. Mark my words, Olivia, nothing will ever replace a good book."

As we drew closer to the Frisco railroad tracks my stomach started to churn. When we bounced over the two iron rails, I held by breath, my hat, and crossed my fingers. Once we had traveled a short way into Tulsa, the number of horse-drawn wagons seemed to be about equal to the new gasoline-powered modes of transportation. Along with the posted bills on storefronts advertising cold beer and haircuts, were large black and white signs that read, "Whites Only. NO Colored Allowed".

A sign hanging in the window of O'Brian's Saloon read, "No Dogs, No Negros, No Mexicans. No Kidding". I turned toward Mister Swede, pointed to the despicable message. "I wonder if Mister O'Brian would sell me a bucket of beer? The sign doesn't say no to Indians.

"I suppose you could claim your Red Man heritage, but I'm of the opinion Mister O'Brian would find a way to say no. Try as much as you might, Olivia, I'm afraid we'll never understand what provokes racial prejudice."

"Maybe some folks are just born that way like a curse on their souls."

Mister Swede didn't refute my comment. He looked at the street sign, made a hard-left turn, then reined in the bay.

"Why, Olivia," he said, turning his attention to me. "You look positively green around the gills. Now, now, girl...chipper upper. When I was a young lad and afraid to board a lorry, my dear mother asked me, 'Horace, what is there to fear except fear itself?'"

My voice was barely a whisper when I replied, "I swore that I'd never step one foot over the Frisco railroad tracks. Negros are not wanted in these parts. Why did I even come here?"

Mister Swede started climbing down off the surrey. "You came to apply for a job. And you'll succeed. Remember that."

When both of us were standing on the front porch of a ramshackle shotgun house with rusted tin covering the roof, Mister Swede pulled out his pocket watch. "It's exactly 9:00 a.m." He then carefully placed his gold-plated watch back in his vest pocket. He turned to give me a half-baked smile. "Go ahead, Olivia, knock on the door."

First, I made sure the starched white cotton blouse I wore was properly tucked into the waist of my ankle-length, gray wool skirt. A matching gray bonnet had been securely pinned to my hair. I knocked and when the door opened, I stood face-to-face with a middle-age man wearing a food-stained undershirt and a pair of baggy khaki trousers.

"I don-a wan' any," he said and slammed the door in my face.

I looked at Mister Swede, who shrugged, and said, "Try, try, again."

I knocked on the door and waited. This time, when it swung open, before the man could get a word in edgewise, I said, "Salve signore. Il mio nome è Olivia Truluck. Sono qui per fare domanda per il lavoro di traduttore."

The man smiled, exposing an uneven row of tobacco-stained teeth. "Okay, okay. Why don'-a you-a no say so?"

Once Mister Swede and I were inside, we were directed to sit on a horse-hair hump-back sofa. My interviewer sat on a cane-bottom chair positioned directly across from me. He stuck a stubby black cigar in his mouth that was already half chewed and nodded, which I took as my cue.

"My qualifications for the translator job are as follows - I've completed the beginner and intermediate programs in conversational Italian and am currently working on the advanced course. I'm a graduate from Mister Swede's Normal School and I'm available for immediate employment as a translator. Capire?"

My prospective employer looked at me while wallowing the cigar stub from side-to-side in his mouth. Finally, he removed the black stogie and spit in a coffee can acting as a spittoon sitting on the floor next to his chair. He wiped a hand on his trousers, then held it out for a shake. Instead of removing my brown leather gloves like most men would do, I kept them on while shaking his hand.

"Okay. You're hired. You start next-a week."

The fast pace of the interview left me searching for words. Mister Swede filled in the blanks. "Ah…Sir, may we inquire as to the duties Miss Truluck will be asked to perform…and your name, please?"

The man grinned and stuck the unlit cigar back in his mouth. He pointed to his chest. "I'm John Pusateri, but everybody, they call me Banana John. I come here with the produce." Banana John looked up at me and nodded. "The girl, she helps me with the customers, no?"

"You're a green-grocer, is that it?" Mister Swede asked.

Banana John shrugged. "Green-grocer – I dunno what that is. I'm from Saint Louie where my brother, Giuseppe, he will ship produce to Tulsa."

"So," I said, finally finding my voice, "you want me to work in your grocery store. Is that right, Mister Pusateri?"

"No, no. I'm trying to tell-a you. I don't have no grocery store. I sell the produce to the grocery store, capire?"

I nodded and asked, "May I ask, what will be my compensation for performing the translator duties?"

"We donna' put a price on you yet. We wait and see what you can do for Banana John."

CHAPTER THIRTEEN
TAKE ME OUT TO THE BALLGAME

After recrossing the Frisco railroad tracks, Mister Swede hurried the surrey past the Dimebox Movie Theater without comment. When I arrived home, Mama was in the kitchen priming the handpump. I took over the task as she went back to scrubbing pots and pans.

I picked up a clean towel to dry the dishes, and said, "I got the job."

Mama looked tired, but her voice was still chipper. "That's wonderful, Olivia. Where will you be working, Darlin'?"

"On a produce wagon," I replied, wiping the water drops from Mama's favorite mixing bowl.

Mama stopped to take a swipe at the beads of perspiration that had formed on her forehead. In the process she left soap suds clinging to her hair. "You'll be lumping produce? I thought the advertisement said translator."

"It did. Banana John delivers produce to grocery stores, like yours. He doesn't speak English very well and he has a lot of trouble with numbers. He's looking for someone like me, who can speak both languages and do the math, too. My job will be to make sure that Mister Banana John does not get raked by his customers. You could call me a middle-man, or woman. As far as his math deficiencies, I'm going to teach him how to add, subtract and multiply." I gave Mama a big confident smile. "Banana John calls himself a 'pigeon' because unscrupulous clients are taking advantage of the 'skunky' situation."

When Mama looked at me, her smile evaporated. "Olivia, if working for this Banana John man means you are going to start talking like a common stevedore, then I'll have to forbid to you take the job. All these new words like 'hot dang' 'hubba-hubba' and 'gee whiz' - they're just not an appropriate use of the English language."

"But Mama. Mister Swede said this job would be a wonderful opportunity for me not only to use my language skills, but to learn how to communicate with white people." Without a word Mama went back to washing dishes. I ran out of the kitchen, found my purse where I left it and hurried back to where Mama was still bent over the sink.

"Mama, look."

She turned around and gasped. "Why, Olivia, it's a banana."

"My new boss gave it to me."

I peeled the rare yellow fruit and held it out for Mama to pinch off the very first bite. Just the two of us devoured that entire banana while giggling like a couple of monkeys in a zoo. Mama reached out with her strong arms and gave me a big hug. "Child, I want you to remember that corruption finds a dozen alibis for its evil deeds. If that Banana man is getting 'skinned' by his customers, make sure you have long ears, big eyes and a short tongue."

****

Although the baseball game was scheduled to begin at 2:00 p.m., I was waiting on the front porch raring to go an hour early. When Mama finally decided to come out of the house, I knew by the way she adjusted the cameo pinned high on her collar that she was fit to be tied.

I kept my voice neutral when I asked, "Mama, are you sure you want to go? I mean, watching a baseball game sound so boring. I'm sure there are a million things you'd rather be doing."

"Are you ready, Olivia?"

"Yes, Mama."

As we walked along Greenwood Avenue, Mama looked at me out of the corner of her eye. "Olivia, I will not allow you to attend a sporting event without a proper chaperone. All manner of undesirable people show-up at those...those baseball games."

When the two of us arrived at the baseball field, the game

had already begun. There were over one-hundred or more spectators already lined up behind a waist-high picket fence. Mister James Bingham was decked out in a white baseball uniform with black pin-striping and black stockings. Like the star of a vaudeville act, he was center stage, positioned on a low mound of red dirt, bent over at the waist, glaring at the batter. Then, like an octopus unravelling its tentacles, James was a blur of arms and legs. After throwing the speeding projectile, it smashed into the catcher's leather glove making a popping sound.

Mama nudged my shoulder. "That man throwing the baseball, I take it he's your Mister Bingham?"

"Yes, Ma'am," I replied. "Isn't he the cat's meow?"

Mama didn't smile but I could tell she was a mite impressed. "I wonder if he's as smart as he is handsome."

The batter positioned himself at the plate, took a couple of practice swings and nodded. The pitching and swishing ended when "Strike three" was called. The batter threw his bat on the ground, kicked up a cloud of red dust and stalked off the field, mumbling curse words over his shoulder. Everyone started wildly clapping yelling and whistling. I did too, but not Mama.

Mister Bingham finally glanced in my direction. My cheeks turned red. Embarrassed, I looked down at my feet. When I looked up, he gave me a big smile and doffed his cap. Once the game was over, a mob of people rushed out onto the field. The baseball players shook hands with the fans and autographed baseballs. James finally pulled away from the crowd of admirers. He slowly walked over to where Mama and I were standing under the shade of a sweet-smelling sycamore tree.

"Miss Truluck," he said, taking his baseball cap off and tipping it in my direction. "I'm so glad you came today." He looked over at Mama and gave her a million-dollar smile. "And this must be...your sister, I assume?"

"Oh, no," I gasped, my knees suddenly going weak.

"I'm her mother," Mama said.

"That's right," I twittered.

James bowed at the waist and held out his hand. "Pleased to meet you, Missus Truluck. I'm James O. Bingham."

Mama extended her arm and shook hands with James. Her tone was curt but not hostile when she acknowledged his presence. "Mister Bingham."

"Please excuse my earlier attempt at a joke, Missus Truluck. I know this may sound presumptuous but, one day, I'm going to marry your daughter."

****

Sometimes life moves at such lightning-speed it takes your breath away, other times it's so slow you'd think tomorrow will never come. It was twelve long months after that baseball game that I became a married woman. Mister James O. Bingham and I didn't just jump the broom, we flew over it. My dear husband and I decided to forgo a honeymoon. Instead, we pooled my dowry money, with his recent inheritance from a deceased uncle, and a small loan from Father, to purchase property from Mister J. B. Stratford. While our new home was under construction, James and I lived with Father and Mama Rose. It wasn't the best place for newly-weds but it would have to do.

It was noon one bright, sunny Sunday. Three Trulucks, two Binghams, and one Mister Swede were gathered around Mama's kitchen table. We had finished a sumptuous meal of fried chicken, potatoes au gratin, wilted spinach, and raw oysters. We were ready to dig into a cherry pie that I'd made from the fruit canned last summer.

James leaned back in his chair to crow, "Will you just look at my talented wife? Ain't she the sweetest thing since cane sugar?"

Mama looked at me and grunted. "From the looks of your beautiful wife's belly I'd say she's cooked up more than a cherry pie."

James' face beamed brighter than a hundred-watt incandescent lightbulb. "That's right, Mama. We intend to give our boy everything he needs to live a happy life."

"Tell me, dear husband," I said, placing a hand over my ever-protruding stomach. "What if it's a girl?"

James reached over to place his hand on top of mine, "Honor bright, Darlin'. It'd be just the same."

Mama nodded in agreement and pointed at the half-eaten cherry pie. "I noticed that Olivia has taken more interest in her domestic duties." Mama placed a fork on her empty dessert plate and gave me a serious look. "Olivia, how long do you intend to keep working for Banana John?"

I shrugged. "Until I can't. My work is all mental."

James removed his hand from mine after gently patting my

stomach. "I say it's time to give Banana John your resignation. The man should be able to add and subtract by now, right?"

"Oh, James, I don't do any heavy lifting. Besides, we need the money to finish our new house."

From one end of the table there came a familiar voice. "There's terrible news from Atlanta, Georgia." Mister Swede pointed at the Sunday newspaper he'd been holding inches from his face in order to see the words. "White people have taken to the streets. Negros have been hung from lampposts. Over twenty men and women stabbed or shot to death. Negro homes and businesses burned to the ground. This is terrible, I tell you, just terrible. Have we learned nothing since emancipation?"

"That doesn't sound like a riot, more like a massacre," I said.

"Does the article say why it happened?" Father asked.

Mister Swede shook his head. "I fear whatever excuse is given it will not be the truth. Economic times are tough. Jobs are scarce and competition is fierce. Employers pay little or next to nothing for a day's labor. If a union is formed the members are fired, beaten or worse."

"They'll blame all that violence on some Negro," James said, shaking his head. "Maybe it was just for looking at a white woman cross-eyed."

"The Negro people in Atlanta should form their own business district," Father said. "Just like we did here in Greenwood. I do believe that the separation of the races is the only way we'll ever find peace."

Jerome looked over at Father to ask, "What happened in Atlanta will never happen here, right?"

Father shrugged and said in a hushed voice, "Jobs are plentiful here."

"Only as long as the oil keeps flowing," Mama offered.

"It's gushing now," Father reminded all of us. "As a matter of fact, James will be working with me on the oil rigs this winter. Right, James?"

"Yessir. My arm will get quite a workout with a three-pound hammer." James turned to me. "What's wrong, Olivia? You've got that crabbed look on your face."

"Is everything okay with the baby?" Mama asked in a worried voice.

Instead of an answer, I smiled and served James another slice of pie. There was no sense worrying the family about all of the turmoil, besides the unborn baby, that was churning around inside my stomach. The daily obstacles I faced as an American Negro were universal in this country, so there really wasn't anything anyone could do to help.

CHAPTER FOURTEEN
HARD LABOR

Although I'd been working for Banana John for almost a year some of his customers still balked at my participation, even hinting I wasn't welcome inside their store. But my boss insisted that my presence was necessary and that without Banana John there would be none of his always fresh produce. It was our last stop of the day when Banana John applied the wagon's handbrake, turned to me and asked, "What is Mister Rudloff's order?"

I turned the pages of the big green ledger on my lap until I came to the one with the heading, "Rudloff's Grocery". "A box of navel oranges, the little sweet ones, not the big ones that are sour and taste like grapefruits. Half a bunch of bananas without bruises, a hundred-pound sack of russet potatoes with no rust or deep-set eyes, and one case of crisp head lettuce, not the limp, wilted kind."

While Banana John was unloading the produce, I was urged to find some relief for my overflowing bladder. With the fetus rolling around inside my belly, he or she had one foot stuck in my ribs and the other one was kicking my spleen. I held my water, telling myself, "You didn't wet your pants when the K.K.K. burned down your house and you'll persevere, now. I slowly eased my bloated body off the wagon. Concentrating, I held my knees together and duck-walked all bent over toward the backdoor of Rudloff's. I stepped inside and had to stop for a moment to let my eyes adjust to the darkness. Then, I saw someone moving in the corner.

When the shadow started moving toward me, I asked, "Mister Rudloff?" There wasn't an answer. I froze as the dark shape drew nearer. It was only Mister Rudloff's teenage son, so I let my guard down.

"I...I know your restroom is for whites only, but I have to use it really bad."

"That's not okay." The brawny kid lurched toward me so close I could smell his alcohol-saturated breath. That made me almost lose my lunch, especially when the red festering pimple on his long nose started oozing pus. He growled, "If I let you use it what's in it for me?"

"I'm sorry?"

He leaned even closer to whisper in my ear, "You niggers are all the same. Ain't nothin' fer' free. Why can't you get it? If you want to use my shitter then you gotta' give me somethin' in return. It's only fair. Or, you can go outside and piss. I won't watch, promise."

Without warning, the man-boy aggressively wrapped an arm around my waist. With my heart beating triple time. I reared back and hissed, "Stop."

In an instant the stinking human weight was pulled off of me. Banana John was holding the aggressor by the scruff of his neck. "What the hell is the matter wit' you? You leave-a this girl alone. You hear what I tell you?"

I fell back against the wall and promptly wet my bloomers. Old man Rudloff walked in about this time and relented to let me have free use of the "Whites Only" restroom. Banana John added ten-dollars to Mister Rudloff's produce bill for my metal pain and anguish. When my boss and I were back in the wagon heading home, he looked over at me.

"You okay?"

"Yes," I said, trying to keep my voice under control.

"I dunno what's a matter with the kids these days. They act worse than monkeys in-a the zoo. Like they lost their brains."

"That's the first time I've ever been called a nigger." My voice was soft and low when I asked, "I wonder, what exactly is a nigger? Is it only someone whose skin is black?"

Wallowing the ever-present cigar stub from one side of his mouth to the other, my boss answered, "A nigger is somebody who's looked upon as a worthless, lazy no-account. Like-a Rudloff's kid. The word don't apply to skin color."

I reached across and squeezed Banana John's arm. "I'm so

glad you were there to help me, Mister Pusateri. Thank you."

We rode most of the way home in silence, until Banana John shook his head vigorously. "The way white folks here in Tulsa treat Negros, it's-a shameful. Not right at all. From now on, this Banana John only sell his produce to-a the Negros in-a the Greenwood District." He turned to me with a broad smile. "Maybe I'll open me a little grocery store, too, eh?"

"I don't think you can," I said. "White people aren't allowed to own a business in the Greenwood District."

Banana John chuckled, and said, "We'll-a see. We'll-a see."

****

That evening, after supper I sat alone on the back porch. It was candle lighting time. The lilac bush I'd planted near the outhouse had grown into a tree with large beautiful purple blooms. I rubbed my ever-swelling belly and hoped whoever was rolling around inside was a girl. James wanted a male heir, but eventually boys leave their family, while girls are more inclined to stay close to home, just like I did. If the child is of the female variety then I could show her how to build a nest in the lilac tree and we could have a proper tea party. I suppose if it was a boy we could build a fort.

While day-dreaming about my old hiding place in Missouri under the lilac tree, Mama came outside. She took a seat beside me and fired-up Father's corncob pipe. She said the tobacco aided her digestion and settled the sand. Up to that point in time, I never knew Mama had a nervous condition that needed settling. Her motto had always been "Live in worry and die in a hurry".

Mama pulled out the tobacco pouch tucked in her big white apron and after filling the pipe's bowl, she struck a wooden kitchen match on her thumbnail, calmly took a couple of puffs on the pipe and nodded toward the outhouse.

"Would you look at that lilac bush. With all the rain. I bet it's grown two feet this year."

"Mama, how tall is that lilac bush?"

Mama leaned forward to squint. "Looks to be taller than the outhouse."

"Uh-huh. Then I guess we better start calling it a tree."

Mama chuckled and took another puff. She tried to blow smoke rings in the air, but the soft breeze sept them away. She finally gave up and asked, "What's the matter with my girl?"

89

I shook my head. "Nothing."

"Don't you fib to me. I was watching you this evening at dinner. Why, you barely touched your food. And whenever James looked at you, instead of smiling and blushing, you looked away. At one point I thought you were going to cry."

That's when the dam broke. I couldn't stop the tears from flowing and my shoulders from shaking. Mama reached out and pulled me close. "C'mon, now, Olivia. Tell Mama what's wrong."

After I stopped sniffing and blew my nose on one of Mama's ever-present clean cotton handkerchiefs, I whispered, "Today, something horrible happened. If it hadn't been for Banana John, I hate to think what he would have done."

Mama pulled me in closer to her body. "Are you hurt, sugar?" I shook my head "no". "Then, that's it. You ain't goin' back across those railroad tracks. Not tomorrow. Not next week or next month. Not never-more. Those ill-mannered white people just can't be trusted to do the right thing."

"I won't have to cross the tracks anymore, Mama. Banana John said he's not selling to whites, only to Negros. He says he wants to open a store here in Greenwood."

Mama slowly relaxed her hold on me, then drew her head back to give me a good long look. Finally, after giving my comment much thought, she said, "You see, Olivia. Like I've always told you, there's a bright sun behind every dark cloud."

"What do you mean, Mama?"

"Banana John can't open a grocery in Greenwood, but he can be my silent partner. We'll stock his produce in my store on consignment and he can sell to the other Negro grocers in town. Our prices will be lower, and we won't have to invest a penny in produce inventory. We'll split the profits fifty-fifty with Banana John."

I looked at Mama and shook my head. "Mama, you are so smart when it comes to running a business. Where did you learn to do that?"

"Child, business is a lot like evolution."

"You mean Darwin's theory?"

"Uh-huh," Mama grunted and nodded. "That's Mama's theory, too. Adapt or else."

"There's just one more thing, Mama. I...I haven't told James about what happened at Rudloff's today."

Mama knocked the spent ashes out of her pipe and shook her head. "Olivia, life goes on no matter what we try to do to change it. No harm was done, except to your bloomers and your pride. James has enough on his plate these days. No need for him to be worrying over an ignorant white man you'll never see, again."

****

Ignoring the pain that started in my lower back pain region, my protruding stomach was always in the way along with the constant urge to relieve myself. James and I moved into our new home over the Christmas holidays. January twenty-second, 1907 began with a dry blue norther'. The gale raged constant all day and blew even harder throughout the night. At sunrise the next morning the wind was calm. Outside, the sky was cloudless and the water in the bird bath looked to be frozen solid. I was dressed in a frumpy house-robe and had a fire going in the new Lattimer-Williams Stove, when James came into the kitchen.

He gave me a peck on the cheek and took a seat at our round oak pedestal table. While waiting for the water to boil, my husband asked, "Had another rough night, did you? Want me to rub your back?"

I redirected my swollen ankles toward my husband, popped the bones in my spine. "James, I'm just worn down and worn out. For just one minute, I wish you could get inside my body and be me."

"Why, if I could do that, I'd tell that baby to come out, come out, whoever you are."

Gently, James placed a hand on my stomach and looked up at me with a honey coated smile. "I think the little booger has found a permanent home. Mama Rose suggested you walk three miles a day and eat more sauerkraut."

"Just the thought of that horrible stuff makes me want to throw-up."

Once the water was at a rolling boil, I spooned in six tablespoons of black coffee, let the piping hot liquid work for a minute, then using a kitchen strainer, filled James' cup. He blew on the rising steam then took a tiny sip of the boiling black brew. He made a sour-looking face and carefully placed the blue cup back on the matching saucer.

"What's in this coffee – ground tree bark?"

I thought about letting the comment slide but due to my

delicate condition, I was edgy and snapped, "Chicory."

"Uh-huh," James grunted. "Maybe you should stick with the Hill Brothers Vacuum Packed Coffee like Mama Rose sells at the grocery."

"Maybe if you want your coffee made any different, maybe you should roll out of bed at five a.m. and make it yourself."

The next words out of my mouth would have been "I'm not your slave", but that comment was never mentioned, because at that exact moment my water broke.

****

Several minutes later I was inside my bedroom, laying on the four-poster brass bed looking up at Mama. She took my hand in hers and gave me the sweetest smile.

"How are we feeling, Dear?"

"Like I'm ready to pass a...a..."

Suddenly, another contraction hit. I reached up with both hands and grabbed the brass rails on the bed's headboard. As the pain eased and my breath was under control, I whispered, "a watermelon."

"Now, Olivia," Mama said, "I want you to just lay there and try to make yourself comfortable."

I laughed and paid for it with a sharp pain in my left side. Mama handed me a clean cotton towel that had been tied into a knot. "If those pains get to be too much for you, bite down on this. It'll save your teeth. I'd give you some chamomile tea to ease the pain but I'm afraid it might harm the baby."

"That's, okay, Mama," I said, griping the towel when another contraction hit. "I just want you to know that if something goes wrong, you save my baby first, promise?"

"Olivia, I'll not have that kind of talk. Once it's over, you and the baby will be just fine."

"But, Mama, do you remember last month, when that woman who lives two doors down was in labor?"

Mama nodded. "Yes, Dear. There were complications, but she was much older than you. The midwife saved her life."

"But her baby died," I whispered, and looked up at Mama. "If that happened to my baby, I wouldn't want to live anymore."

CHAPTER FIFTEEN
DEATH DECLARES NO HOLIDAY

There I lay, sprawled out on my back like a beached seal, with my legs spread wide apart. I could barely see the top of Mama's head over my protruding belly. She was squatting at the end of the bed and when I lifted my head up, I could see that Mama's face was all scrunched up like something was going wrong with the delivery.

"What is it Mama?"

"Nothing, Olivia. Nothing at all."

"There must be," I cried out between contractions. "My God, there has to be a better way to procreate the human species. Pushing another human out a woman's vagina is cruel and unusual punishment. Oh Lord, what is taking the baby so dang long to come out?"

There was worry etched on her forehead when Mama looked at me. "Olivia, this little critter is trying to come out butt first. I'm gonna' try to turn it around."

"Please, Mama. Just do something, anything, please."

"Olivia, calm down. Remember to keep breathing or you'll pass out."

"Good. Wake me when it's over."

"We're gonna' get you through this. All it takes is some grit an' I know you got plenty of that. Think about something pleasant, like your nest under the old lilac tree."

At that exact moment another contraction hit. Worse than any that came before, it was like heavyweight boxing champion, John L. Sullivan, had punched me in the gut. I bit down hard on the knotted towel and tried to control my breathing. The sound of Mama's voice seemed far away.

"Olivia, I'm gonna' use some lard, but this will still hurt some. You bite down hard on that towel, girl. We don't want you to ruin any of those pretty teeth of yours."

I groaned and chewed on that towel. Mama stuck two, three or maybe all five fingers, up my vagina to reposition and redirect the baby. Finally, when she was satisfied everything was aligned, including the stars and planets, Mama raised her head up.

"All right, Olivia. It's ready to drop. Now, I want you to roll off slowly and squat next to the bed."

"But, Mama," I whined, as she helped me move, "I don't have anything left to pee."

"I know that, Dear. We're going to deliver this child the Indian way."

I did as Mama directed, squatted on my haunches, leaned back against the iron bed frame and put my hands up on Mama's shoulders for support. Mama sat cross-legged on the floor in front of me. She placed her elbows at her side, held her hands together with her palms up under my pelvis, and directed me to, "Push."

"Mama," I croaked. "You better use James' catcher's mitt."

"Olivia," Mama barked. "Pay attention. Now, I want you to push. Hard. Now."

I did push, harder than I'd ever pushed before, then I heard Mama cry, "Lord a mercy. It's a homerun".

****

When Mama allowed James and Father to enter my bedroom the baby and I were snuggled under a goose down comforter. Mama proudly stood next to the bed with her chest all puffed out. The two men tiptoed into the room talking in whispers.

"Why the worried look, Simon," Mama asked.

"Well, Rose, there was a whole lot of catterwaulin' goin' on in here. We didn't know if maybe Olivia was having dire straits."

"Looks to me like Olivia's doing just fine," James said softly. He came over to kneel next to me. "Are you okay, Sugar?"

"A little sore, but yes I'm okay. Do you want to hold her?"

Like he was holding a delicate porcelain doll, James cradled the baby in his arms. As he rocked his daughter side to side, immense joy radiated from his eyes. He looked at the baby and asked, "Got a name little one?"

I reached out and patted James's arm. "I thought I'd give you the honor."

He thought for a moment then said, "Alicia. That was my mother's name."

"Good," I said, closing my eyes and drifting off to sleep. "Alicia it is then."

****

A year and a day had gone by since James buried Alicia's afterbirth under the lilac tree next to the outhouse. Although, some of my girlfriends warned of negative feelings after childbirth, I didn't have time to wallow in postpartum depression. Mama needed my help at the store. I was in the back of the grocery store surrounded by boxes and cases of canned-goods. It was a hot afternoon in mid-July. I was nursing Alicia when the telephone rang.

"Rose's Grocery," Mama said, answering the call and giving me a big smile of happiness. I returned the show of affection and watched as Mama's smile slowly faded then completely disappeared. Mama had been silent during the short telephone conversation, muttering only a "yes" or "no". When she placed the receiver back in its cradle, Mama let her body sink down on a stool behind the counter.

"What is it, Mama?"

Unable to form coherent words, she wrung her hands and stared up at me. Finally, with trembling lips, Mama said, "At the wellhead. Simon slipped and fell…"

"No Mama…Not Daddy."

She nodded. I placed Alicia in her bassinet and went over to put my arms around Mama's broad shoulders. We held each other, rocking back and forth, until she pulled back. When Mama looked at me there was an indescribable sorrow in her teary eyes.

"Olivia, right now we've got no time to grieve. I'll take care of the customers then we'll close for the day. Tomorrow, Banana John can run the place. You take Alicia home and wait until I come for you."

"James," I said. "He's on the road, somewhere in Texas. I

95

need him here now, with me."

"Don't worry, Dear," Mama said, lifting my chin with her hand. "I'll have Mister Swede contact his manager."

I stood motionless, staring at Mama, tears dripping off my cheeks. Mama hugged me tight, again. Her demeanor appeared stoic, but her voice cracked when she said, "It'll be alright, Olivia. Your Daddy's at peace now and the rest of us have to go on living."

****

The wake was held in Mama's parlor. I sat dry-eyed next to Mama, unable to tear my eyes away from the coffin. With no boo-hooing some might have thought I didn't care about losing my father. Little did they know that I'd already cried out all my tears the night before. Father was clad in his good black suit and a white shirt with a collar. He was laid out in an oak Eternity box that he'd built with dove-tail boards guaranteed not to leak for one-hundred years, or at least until Jesus Christ made His big comeback. Flickering light from the burning tapers situated on both sides of the coffin reflected off the gold wedding band on Father's left hand that was neatly laid across his chest. I remember those same strong, rough hands comforting me, no matter what. Huge bouquets of flowers indigenous to central Oklahoma surrounded him in urns, vases and baskets. Banana John, dressed discreetly in a black suit, minus the cigar, handed both Mama and me a white lily and like a native Sicilian, kissed her on both cheeks.

Finally, I summoned the nerve to walk over to the coffin and look down at the man I loved just as much as my husband but in a different way. Compared to the giant-of-a-man he was when alive, now Daddy looked half his size. His eyes were sewn shut and his lips, once full and thick, were two thin ribbons of dark skin. The workers who brought Father home in a wagon told us that he was on top of a fifty-foot oil rig, when he slipped and fell, breaking his neck. I thought it odd that except for a blue goose egg on his forehead, there wasn't a mark on his face.

I touched his hand and whispered, "I love you, Daddy. And I'll always remember you."

The tears attacked, again. I stood alone weeping, until James came up and put his arm around me. "Your Daddy was a good man, Olivia. At work, not once did I ever hear him raise his voice in anger. Even when the others were loud, or griping and complaining about one thing or another, Simon was always the calming voice of reason."

James escorted me into the next room. Mama's round oak table groaned under the weight of a twenty-pound turkey and a roasted piglet with an apple stuck in its mouth. To stay busy and keep my brain in neutral during this ordeal, I had baked four pumpkin pies.

I looked at my husband, and asked, "You're hungry, aren't you?"

"I could eat."

I cut a generous wedge of pumpkin pie and placed it on a plate. When I offered it to James, he took it and asked, "Aren't you going to have piece with me?"

"Not right now. I'm not hungry."

James made short work of my culinary effort. "Delicious," he said, and kissed my cheek. "Just the right amount of sugar, from my Sugar."

"I made pumpkin because it was Daddy's favorite. Now it looks like it's yours, too."

"A man has to keep up his strength," James said, rubbing his stomach. He looked at me for a moment then took my hands in his. "So does a woman."

"All I need is time. Don't worry, I'll eat, again. It's just that I wasn't ready for something like this to happen. Everything was bright and sunny. Now a dark cloud has fallen over us. I didn't think, I never even imagined, that anything like this could change my happy world."

James kissed the tops of my hands. "Death comes unexpected and takes whoever it wants. In the meantime, you and I? We'll only count the sunny days."

James encircled me with his strong arms and pulled me close. It was the first time since hearing the horrible news about Daddy that I felt a sense of peace.

CHAPTER SIXTEEN
MULE HEADED

O, happy day. On November 16, 1907, the Oklahoma Territory became the 46th state to enter the union. That night, the skies above both sides of the Frisco railroad tracks were illuminated with a profusion of multi-colored fireworks. I think Mister Swede spoke for all the Trulucks when he said, "It's been forty-three years since the unpleasantness between the states. Now, if all Oklahomans can come together, I foresee a time when Negros will be welcomed into Tulsa's white businesses and Negro children will attend schools with their white counterparts."

The only reply was from Mama, who said, "Does that mean we'll have to let white people own businesses in the Greenwood District?"

Up until that time, I never gave much thought to the idea that the Negros in Greenwood were practicing a reverse form of discrimination. A smile crossed my lips before I muttered, "Well if you ask me, they started it and I don't think we can ever be friends. Negro and white children learning their a, b, c's in the same classroom? I really don't see it happening."

Turkey day came and went without a word of reconciliation from the people of Tulsa or its politicians. The week before Christmas, Mister Swede, James, and I sat around the table in my kitchen watching chestnuts roast over an open fire.

"Did you soak the nuts in brine first?" Mister Swede asked.

"No," I replied. "Why do that?"

Mister Swede shrugged. "Soaked in brine the roasted chestnuts would be pre-salted."

James sat off to the side carving a wooden doll's head for Alicia's Christmas present. "I'd like to soak their all of their chestnuts in kerosene," James groused.

"And just whom are you referring to, Dearest," I asked. "Elected officials, every one of them they're all nothing but low-class scoundrels, all the way to the bone."

"I concur, James," Mister Swede said, as he held a burning taper to the bowl of a briar pipe. He held the stem fast between his clenched teeth, puffing huge plumes of smoke in my general direction. Then the wise old tutor cleared his throat and said, "Our esteemed state legislators, a most despicable group of village idiots. Once they were sworn-in - what was their first order of business?" Without waiting for an answer, Mister Swede continued. "They passed a law legitimizing segregation. That's right folks, Jim Crow can fly with impunity over the state of Oklahoma."

"It's always one step forward and two steps back," I groused.

James sat stiff as a ramrod and shrugged. "The white man holds all the aces. That means he makes all the laws. Ain't nothin' so unusual about that, now is there, Mister Swede?"

I nodded in agreement with James' observation, moved Alicia from the empty breast to the full one, and asked, "Please, Mister Swede, can you tell us something we don't know?"

"I can tell you that in this month alone there were over six-hundred coal miners, Negros and whites, killed in two separate explosions. The continued exploitation of the working class by the Capitalist oligarchs cannot continue not if this country wants peace. I've officially joined the Socialist Party. We meet in May of next year to nominate our candidate for president and I assure you it'll be someone who will defeather Mister Jim Crow."

"And just who would that someone be?" I asked.

"Eugene Debs."

A visibly agitated Mister Swede continued to puff on his pipe until the tobacco went cold. He finally rather forcefully thumped the dead ashes out of the intricately carved briar into the palm of his hand, and said, "Be warned there's another movement in this country, one that would take us back, before eighteen-sixty-five."

A chill went up my spine. "You don't mean the reinstitution of slavery, do you?"

"Beware the People's Party, a group of populist nativist who'd like nothing better than to put the Negro race back in chains. I blame the continued degradation of this country, squarely on the shoulders of dime movies. Bah. They're nothing but flummadiddle and contribute nothing."

"Except to the delinquency of minors," James said, and chuckled.

"Mister Swede," I nagged, "that sounds like an elitist attitude."

"If it's snooty to decry immoral films that appeal to the lowest common denominator, then I plead guilty as charged. Commercialism of everything under the sun will lead us all down the path to perdition. Before you know it there'll be advertising billboards on every corner."

James chuckled again and laid the doll head on the kitchen table. "Mister Swede, I think that horse is already out of the barn. There are over ten-thousand nickelodeons in this country four or five right on Greenwood Avenue."

"That's right, Mister Swede," I chined in. "No matter where you look, somebody is trying to sell you something."

"We've got trouble in this town," Mister Swede said, nodding vigorously. "It started with five-cent novels for children and now we're being inundated with flickering images. Before you know it, Thomas Edison will figure out a way to add sound."

Our beloved Mister Swede was becoming hard-of-hearing, not as deaf as Brother Sin-Eater, but enough that a person had to make sure to pronounce every word with emphasis and speak distinctly. It had also become more and more apparent, that my former tutor had become dead-set in his ways. It was impossible to move his opinion, on any subject, in any direction.

"Mister Swede," I said, and pointed to our new mahogany hand-crank gramophone with the large purple horn. "Would you do away with all forms of modern entertainment, even the phonograph?"

"No, no, Olivia, I'm not a total Luddite. I'm saying that if we allow our children to be hypnotized by mere fluff, then they'll be open to any suggestion no matter how obscene or egregious."

****

By the Fourth of July 1908, Eugene Debs was in the running for the November election. The Democratic Party had nominated

William J. Bryan, the Prohibition Party chose Eugene W. Chafin and the Independence Party designated Thomas L. Hisgen to be candidates for President of the United States of America. After all the final votes were tallied, the Republican William H. Taft, received the most electoral votes.

Of course, being a woman and a Negro to boot, I stayed home on election day. I was squatting on my haunches, milking a goat when I heard a rustling sound behind me. The only other animal in the barn besides the nanny was our ancient temperamental Missouri mule, Angel, whose bad habits would make the Devil proud.

I was squeezing the goat's bulging udders, when out of the blue, it felt like somebody had wacked me in the back with a two-by-four. I tumbled forward, screeching, "Ow," then landed face-first on the dirt floor. The pain was horrendous. I rolled over, and when I looked up, sitting on the rafters directly above me were Mister Swede's white and gray homing pigeons.

"Please," I begged. "Don't do it. Not now…please."

I tried to sit up but fell back with a thud. Then, plop, plop, plop.

****

Even though my eyelids were shut tight, I knew the sound of Mama's voice. "I think she's coming around."

"How long has your daughter been unconscious, Missus Truluck?"

"Since yesterday, Doctor."

"Mama," I croaked.

"Yes, Dear?" I felt Mama's cool hand brush against my cheek and stop on my forehead.

Once I was able to pry my eyelids open, everything was blurry. "Where am I?"

"At home, Dear. In your bed."

"Wha-what happened? Where's Alicia?"

"Alicia is fine. Miss Lucy is watching her."

"But…but…she hasn't eaten. I feel like I'm about to bust."

"I know, Dear. But we couldn't bring her until you regained consciousness."

"Your mother is right, Olivia," Doctor Jackson said. "If we had let you nurse your child – I wouldn't want to be responsible for the outcome. It's a known fact that while she's comatose, a mother's milk curdles."

I looked at the doctor, and ordered, "Bring my baby, please."

Once I had Alicia in my arms and she was contently sucking at my breast, I asked, "What happened? I was milking the goat and don't remember--"

Mama shook her head and had a mean look in her eyes. "As far as we can figure, Angel kicked you. I have half a notion to send that dang mule to the glue factory."

"Oh, Mama, the poor beast didn't know what he was doing. He probably thought I was going to hook him up to the hay wagon."

Not one to miss a chance to let loose an old 'saw', Mama said, "The barn wears out an animal quicker than the wagon. Mama sat on the edge of the bed until Alicia was finished nursing. She took the baby in her arms. "The doctor says you should stay in bed and rest. You took a nasty blow. Your backside is all black and blue, but nothing got broken."

"What about chores and the store. If I'm not there, the business..."

Her look was kind and caring. "The business is doin' just fine. Banana John and I can take care of things. What's important is getting you back up on your feet."

"James," I blurted. "He's on the road for the next two weeks. Mama, don't tell him what happened, please."

"Don't you think he'd want to know that you're hurt, Dear?"

I shook my head and lay back down on the pillow. "If he finds out it'll ruin his concentration."

Mama sighed and looked down at her hands. "I know I should bite my tongue, but are you two having disagreements?"

"Oh, Mama," I said, flinging my arm over my eyes. "It's just that he spends so much time on the road. When he is home, all he does is talk about baseball with his friends. Sometimes, I think that he cares more about that stupid game than either me or Alicia."

"Now, now, Dear," Mama whispered, patting my arm. "James is an honest, hard-working man. If his mind is occupied on his job, that's to be expected. Who knows, maybe one of these days your James will play against white men."

"He'd show 'em who's boss," I muttered.

"That's right, Dear. All he wants to do is provide for his family."

"I know, Mama, I know."

She pulled the covers up under my chin and doused the light next to the bed. "You get some rest now and stop lamenting. By tomorrow, you'll be as good as new and back on your feet."

CHAPTER SEVENTEEN
FEVER

It had been a little over a week since I was kicked in the back by the mule. When James returned home from his road trip, he found me laid-up in bed with a thermometer stuck between my lips. Doctor Jackson hovered over me, keeping one eye on his pocket watch and the other on the thin red line of mercury. James quietly sat on the edge of the bed, then placed a cloth that had been soaked in apple cider vinegar on my forehead. Vinegar-soaked towels covered my stomach and my feet. I could hear Mama in the kitchen, chipping away on a block of ice.

"Uh-huh," Doctor Jackson grunted. He held the thermometer up to light streaming through the bedroom window and grunted, again, "Uh-huh." Then, our family doctor with the white goatee looked at me laying there and shook his head. "One-o-two. I thought the Epsom salt bath this morning would take the edge off the fever – but no, as a matter of fact it's gone up a degree."

James looked over at Doctor Jackson. "Kicked by Angel? I'll kill that bastard."

Doctor Jackson shrugged. "Could be, or it could be something else. Fevers are difficult to diagnose. I don't believe shooting the mule would be a bit helpful." The doctor looked at me and asked, "Olivia, didn't you say that while you were on the floor pigeon droppings…ah, fell on you?"

I whispered a weak, "Yes. The stuff was all in my hair."

Doctor Jackson rubbed his chin with a thumb. "Germs could have somehow entered Olivia's bloodstream, maybe from a cut or an open wound. There's blood in her urine, so I'm sure our patient has an infection of some kind, possibly in the kidneys."

"Did you say infection, Doctor?" It was Mama who had just entered the room, carrying a earthenware bowl filled to the rim with chipped ice.

"Yes, I did, Missus Truluck. Pigeon excrement carries a plethora of harmful bacteria. Once it enters the blood-stream the spores can infect any weak organ even attacking the heart."

Mama held a clean white towel under a spoon filled with ice chips. She put the spoon to my lips, looked at me and tried to smile but couldn't rid the worry out of her sad eyes. "If it's an infection, I know just the person who might help."

"Who's that, Mama?" I asked.

"Banana John."

"Mmmmm," Doctor Jackson, hummed. "I better order some leeches."

James patted my hand, and asked, "Doctor Jackson, don't you think we might need a second or maybe a third opinion."

In light of the situation Doctor Jackson agreed. We waited while he made a telephone call to a well-known Negro hospital in Chicago, Illinois. Once the appointment was scheduled, James assured the accounts receivable department that he would pay for all necessary expenses up front. The noted surgeon was to arrive in Tulsa, Oklahoma, by steam locomotive on the Missouri, Kansas and Texas Railroad or KATY for short. When it came to maintaining my health and sanity, I drew the line at attaching leeches to my stomach, but did agree to try Banana John's remedy, a tonic made from fresh garlic, onions, horseradish root and grapefruit along with vinegar and honey. Of course, it tasted just horrible and didn't do a thing to relieve my fever. I was losing weight and when my breasts went dry, a wet nurse was called in for Alicia. Every effort was made to do something, anything to lower my temperature. Mama stuffed chipped ice in hot water bottles, packed them around my body, and turned on an electric table fan.

****

It seemed like forever, but finally, Doctor Patrick Jefferson, the noted Negro surgeon from Provident Hospital in Chicago, Illinois, stood next to my bed. Holding my hand, he looked down at me, his dying patient. I could see the doctor was a sympathetic soul by the blush of true kindness emanating from his eyes. Ever vigilant to my every need, Mama sat by the side of the bed and held a spoon filled with ice chips to my lips.

"Please, Olivia," she begged. "Can you take in just one tiny little piece?" Mama looked up at the doctor and shook her head. "If she doesn't eat something soon...I, don't know."

"Mister Bingham," Doctor Jefferson said, turning toward James. "In your wife's present state, I feel we have to take drastic action and fast. If she loses her will to live and won't eat, then it's all over. I've studied Doctor J. Grasset's Therapy for Maladies. Doctor Grasset devotes a whole chapter to infections, where they come from and how to treat them."

Doctor Jackson asked, "Does Doctor Grasset mention infections of the bloodstream?"

"Yes sir, as a matter of fact he does. He also writes about the internal organs. It is my opinion that Missus Bingham has a bruised kidney that has become infected, resulting in a fever."

"If my child has a bad kidney what can be done?" Mama asked. The burden of worry in her voice made me want to cry, but I didn't have any tears left to shed.

"A nephrectomy," Doctor Jefferson said, his voice low and urgent.

"Remove the kidney?" Doctor Jackson asked. "But the chances of survival are less than..."

"Doctor Jackson," Jefferson said, "please take a look at the bruise on Missus Bingham's lower back. That purple swelling indicates it was the left kidney that took the brunt of the blow. If we don't remove the offending organ, in her frail condition, I'm afraid this woman won't last another week. It's already a proven fact. One healthy kidney can be sufficient for urine excretion in humans."

"But where will you perform the surgery?" Doctor Jackson asked.

Doctor Jefferson looked around my bedroom, then shrugged. "I'll do it right here, and Doctor Jackson, you will assist."

****

Early the next morning, I lay on my right side, stripped to the waist, waiting for a doctor I barely knew, who was going to cut me open with a sharp surgical instrument and remove my diseased kidney. While I lay there wondering why there was no third or fourth opinion, Doctor Jefferson and Doctor Jackson discussed how best to render me unconscious.

Doctor Jefferson admitted, "Too much chloroform and the patient dies, too little and they feel all the pain."

"Why not use ether?" Doctor Jackson suggested. "It's much safer than chloroform."

"It's also much slower and not as effective," Doctor Jefferson replied. "Under normal conditions, I'd use ether as an anesthetic, but this is not a usual procedure. Chloroform is more potent than ether which ensures that the patient feels no adverse results before, during and shortly after surgery."

"Pray God, she's still alive," Doctor Jackson muttered, seemingly not concerned that I was laying right in front of him.

I could hear the clanking of Doctor Jefferson's surgical instruments as he shuffled through them. "Doctor Jackson, keep a close observation on Missus Bingham's pulse and her breathing, I'll administer the chloroform in low concentrations with an atomizer until we're absolutely sure that she's asleep."

As the voices faded into the background, the last thing I remember seeing was seeing Mama walk toward the bed, carrying a handful of bulging hot-water bottles. I have no recollection, nor can I accurately describe what it felt like to be sliced open from sternum to backbone, then have someone stick their hand inside your body cavity to remove an internal organ, because fortunately, Doctor Jefferson administered the exact amount of chloroform according to my body weight and I was out like I'd been hit in the head with one of James' one-hundred-mile-per-hour curve balls.

****

Exactly one month after the successful nephrectomy, my stitches had been removed and I was back at Rose's Grocery operating with one kidney and two good hands. James was toiling in the oil fields, while Mister Swede's Normal School enrollment swelled to such a large number of students, he had to hire two more tutors. And Jerome? My brother never came home that Christmas but returned to the Greenwood District to celebrate Easter 1909.

I heard the familiar 'A-hoo-ga' long before the automobile rolled to a stop on our front lawn. Everyone came running out of the house to inspect the shiny-black Model T. Proudly standing next to his brand-new gasoline powered tin Lizzie, Jerome puffed-up his chest.

"What do ya'll think of my new ride?" Jerome asked with a tip of his derby.

"It's beautiful," I gushed, running my hand over the polished chrome bumper.

"It's all the mustard," James said. "What did it set you back, Jerome?"

"A few hundred bucks but well worth it. Just look at those large rubber tires. No more bouncing around in a hup-mobile for me." Jerome turned toward the Model T and spread his arms wide. "Mark my word, automobiles are the future of transportation. Sell your surrey and buckboard. Put the horses out to pasture, the gasoline-powered automobile is here to stay."

"Applesauce, Jerome," Mama said, wiping her dough-covered hands on her apron. "Where'd you get the money for something fancy like this?"

"I've got a new gig, Mama," Jerome bragged, popping his suspenders and pushing his chest out like he was John D. Rockefeller. "I'm loaded, rollin' in the dough."

Mister Swede lifted the car's hood. He took a minute to inspect the motor, then looked at my brother with a grimace. "Jerome, I do believe you've become persuaded by Ford Motor Company propaganda."

"C'mon, Professor," James said. "Every man needs an automobile with plush leather seats and matching canvas top."

"Bah, humbug," Mister Swede spouted. "Horseless carriages are nothing but toys for rich men. After a ride in one of those contraptions, a contemplative person can't think straight. The power plant under the bonnet is much too complicated for the average man. When something needs repair on your conveyance, and I promise, it will, you're back on shank's mare."

"Don't forget the nasty stuff that comes out the back end," Mama said. "Those fumes smell worse than a dead skunk. Besides, who can afford to feed something so big? They seem to need a constant source of nourishment."

"I beg to disagree, Mama," James said. "I'm of the opinion that automobiles are the wave of the future. When the baseball team is on the road this season, we'll be traveling by bus that's been outfitted with sleeping accommodations. That way, we won't have to search high and low for a place to spend the night."

"Does your new bus include a one-holer, or two-holer?" I asked, balancing Alicia on my hip.

James still knew how to melt my heart when he gave me one of his award-winning smiles. "The good news is, Sweet Cheeks, I won't be on the road as much this coming season. Not if Mister J. B. Stratford has anything to say about it."

"How's that?" Jerome asked, using a clean white handkerchief to remove fingerprints off the right front fender.

"Mister Stratford is financing a new baseball stadium right here in The Greenwood District." James put an arm around Jerome's shoulder. "I'll be pitching for the Greenwood Black Sox."

"James will also be the team's new manager," I added.

Jerome took James's right hand in his and pumped it vigorously up and down. "Good for you, James. Good for you. I brag about you all the time and truth be told, I've won a considerable sum of money betting on your team."

"Why thank you, Brother Jerome," James said.

"Gambling?" Mama cried. "Oh, Jerome, I can't believe you play the Devil's game."

"Now, now, Mama. Take it easy. I'm in the green because of Buddy Bolden, the greatest jazz musician of all time. But Buddy got on that horse called heroin an' rode it right into a New Orleans insane asylum. So now, it's Jerome Truluck who leads the Olympia Band, along with Louis 'Big Eye' Nelson and Joe 'King' Oliver."

"That's wonderful news," Mama gushed and went over to put an arm around Jerome's shoulder. "Not about Buddy, but about your promotion. Now, son, would you please take your tired ol' Mama and the rest of the family out for a little joy ride in your brand-new contraption?"

CHAPTER EIGHTEEN
NEGRO WALL STREET

One afternoon on a sunny spring day in 1914, James and I were strolling down Greenwood Avenue. Along the way we stopped and gawked through the windows of clothing stores, nightclubs and funeral parlors, but kept our eyes focused straight ahead as we hurried past the houses of ill repute. My husband and I were on our way to the offices of Hoakum, Jones and Shirley, located in a two-story brick building in the heart of what had become known as Negro Wall Street.

The electrified hum in the atmosphere came from the sound of people talking at the top of their lungs, angry horses neighing, back-firing, smoke-belching jitneys and the clanging bells of a firetruck. It hadn't occurred to me until that moment that what had once been known as Little Africa now resembled Joplin, Missouri. My escort made a dashing figure to say the least. James was decked-out in his black-on-black tailored wool suit with a starched and ironed white shirt. That's not to mention a shiny new black derby and gray felt spats buttoned at the ankle. He was even carrying a polished ebony walking stick.

James's crowning glory may have been strapped to his feet, but mine was on top of my head. It was a hat made out of red felt. Wide-brimmed and topped with a mountain of tiny rosebuds, I discovered the most annoying part was not the heavy weight but keeping the bees out of my bonnet. My wardrobe was a carbon copy of my husband's, except instead of wool, my black suit jacket and matching trousers were made from velvet. Yes, I do believe we made a handsome couple.

It was a Thursday afternoon and "Maid's day off". James took my hand so we could side-step around the gaggle of women gossiping on the street corner. He pointed in the distance toward Elgin Street.

"Would you look at that? They're almost finished."

"The Booker T. Washington High School," I said.

"I hear they'll enroll over a dozen students."

"Mister Swede's upper school has over twenty students," I bragged, as I stepped off the curb while trying to avoid a pile of road apples.

From behind there came the now familiar A-hoo-ga. Seconds later a topless Model-T roared past. To keep from inhaling the noxious exhaust fumes, I placed one of Mama's handkerchiefs over my nose.

"How many clowns are stuffed in that jitney?" I mumbled.

He chuckled. "Over a dozen I do believe and three hanging on the side." James took my elbow to guide me around a group of loud-mouth teenagers, making nickel bets while shooting craps on the sidewalk.

"Maybe we should buy a jitney," I suggested.

James nodded. "At five-cents a head, we'd make a killing." As we came close to our destination, James and I had to walk the gauntlet where several idle men were lounging against the side of a billiard parlor. I glanced over to see the slicks had a twenty-dollar gold piece hanging from a watch chain. Except for one dandy who flashed two gold front teeth, and ten shiny gold coins attached to a heavy gold watch chain.

Finally, after walking past the new 2 story Williams Dreamland Theater, a movie house that boasted a rooming house on the top floor, James said, "We're here."

Once we were seated inside the office of Mister Harley Hoakum, the founder of Hoakum Jones and Shirley, my husband looked at the wizened old man sitting behind his desk, and flat-out came to terms.

"Mister Hoakum, we're new to this game. We've never invested in stocks."

"That's right," I added, deciding right then and there not to sit silently without offering an opinion. "It's my money, too. I'm not sure we're ready to gamble it away."

Mister Hoakum removed his wire rim glasses, folded the ear-pieces flat and placed them on his desk. "Missus Bingham," he sighed. "There's nothing to worry about. Along with the bank, the stock market is a safe investment with little risk. Banks might fail, but the market will never collapse. The one word motto here at Hoakum, Jones and Shirley is, "Diversify"."

James shifted his weight in the leather-bound chair, and asked, "Mister Hoakum, how did you manage to convince white bankers, who are naturally suspicious of anyone, especially Negros, to front your operation?"

A smile spread across Mister Hoakum's face. "It was the powerful lure of all that Negro green changing hands here in Greenwood. When the scent drifted East to New York, the wheelers and dealers on Wall Street took notice of our all-Negro community. Except for the color of money, Wall Street's brokers and traders are colorblind. They were more than anxious to dip their beaks in our watering hole. Now, we're known as the Negro Wall Street with a direct hook-up to the New York Stock Exchange."

In the end, James and I decided not to invest in stocks, at least not at that very moment. As we exited Mister Hoakum's office that day, I couldn't help but notice all the young Negro men in black button-down coats with a white carnation stuck in their lapel. They were all huddled next to a Morkrum Company teleprinter. For the first time in recorded history, Negro stockbrokers traded equites with their white counterparts. The only hint of envy came from the editorial page of the Tulsa World newspaper. Concerning the Greenwood District's financial success, an jealously-laden article indicated, '…those Negros living north of the Frisco railroad tracks seem to be getting mighty uppity these days'.

****

The Greenwood District's population had swelled to such an extent that Banana John was put in charge of a second, smaller store further south on Greenwood Avenue. Rose's Grocery #2 was close to the Frisco railroad tracks where produce from Saint Louis was unloaded. Due to a condition that Doctor Jackson described as, "The age when a woman goes from vigorous and fertile to tranquil and noble", Mama stayed mostly sidelined by chronic arthritis.

It was late one evening. James and I were sitting in the parlor. He was reading the newspaper while sipping a jigger of whiskey. I sipped a hot toddy and stared vacantly at the painting of an Irish setter hanging on the far wall. My throat was scratchy, and so were my feelings. James and I had been trying hard to conceive another child but without any success. I placed my drink on the side table quietly and turned to look at my husband.

"James?" When he didn't answer, I thought, "The man is either losing his hearing or purposefully ignoring me." I gave him another second to respond, then raised my voice louder. "James?"

He slowly folded the newspaper and turned in my direction. "Yes, Dear?"

"I read the hot springs in Arkansas can increase a woman's fertility."

"So, you want to sit in hot water? Why not let me heat up a kettle on the stove?"

"Don't be a smarter, James."

My husband sighed and leaned in my direction. "C'mon, Sugar. Don't be gettin' upset. One of these days we'll make another baby. Why not look at the bright side? Financially, we're more than well off. Your one kidney does the work of two, and Alicia is smarter than a whip. Not that I thought she wouldn't be."

I tried to give James a nice smile, but I couldn't make my sourpuss face change. "I'm not down in the dumps because we haven't had another child." I picked up a book that was lying on the side table and held it up where James could read the title. "I've been reading this. It's written by Doctor E. H. Starling. He says there are these chemicals in a woman's body called hormones. Doctor Starling says they direct our mood and our feelings. That's why one day I'm happy as a lark and the next as mean as a snark. Don't you see? My disposition is all due to my hormones."

"Uh-uh," James grunted. "Is there a pill you can take for this...mmmm, condition?"

I gave James a sideways glance, wondering if he was still trying to be funny or was taking me seriously. Since he wasn't smiling, I assumed it was the latter. "If you really want to know what's bothering me, I'll tell you."

"I'm listening," he said, taking my hand in his.

I took a deep breath. "Okay then, here goes. James, I've

been doing a lot of thinking. You know, it's been almost twenty years since Idaho and Utah gave white women the right to vote. The rest of the female population, Negro and white, are still disenfranchised."

The expression on James's face said it all. "Yes, Olivia, I know all this. How could I not? You've only told me the same thing dozens of times. But here's the deal, Sweetie, there's not a damn thing neither of us can do about it."

"And I'll keep telling you and anyone who'll stand still to listen that this country practices blatant voter discrimination based on a person's sex and their color."

"Damn, girl," James said, a grin returning to his lips. "You are all riled up about this, aren't you? It must be your hormones stirrin' you up, right?"

"James," I said, taking a deep breath. "Today, I made a rather large monetary donation to the Women's Suffrage Movement. I hope you don't mind."

****

In August of 1916, Horace "Swede" Greely, professor emeritus received the Greenwood Citizen of the Year Award. The honor was bestowed upon the deserving Mister Swede by the Greater Greenwood District Negro Chamber of Commerce. The Chamber's committee decided when it came to race, creed or country of origin they would not discriminate. The prize would go to the person who had dedicated a sizeable amount of time and effort to make Greenwood a better place to live.

It was one week after the award ceremony. Mister Swede and I were occupying box-seats at the new Greenwood District Baseball Park. We were waiting for the game to start. As the home team tossed the ball around, a man who could have passed for a lumberjack strode up to the batter's box. Mister Swede cupped his hands around his mouth and let out a loud Bronx cheer.

"Why, Mister Swede," I gasped. "That's so ill-mannered and rude. What in the world has gotten into you?"

My old tutor, whose hair was nothing but white wisps blowing every which way in the breeze, pointed toward the batter. "I hear their home run hitter crowds the inside of the box. I would hope our Mister Bingham will show him who owns it."

"Don't worry, Mister Swede," I said and patted his light-colored bony hand. "Our Mister James Bingham will dust him right back to St. Louie."

Mister Swede sank back in his seat and nodded. "I must say, Olivia, you certainly have acquired more than an abbreviated knowledge concerning baseball."

"James has taught me all I know about the game. And for the last two years I've been teaching him all about the women's suffrage movement."

"Good for you Olivia. Have you made your yearly contribution?"

I nodded. "Yes sir, I sure have. You know, Professor, when James first found out that I'd donated five-hundred dollars to the cause, he wouldn't speak to me for a week. But finally, after a little persuading, I convinced him it was the right thing to do."

Mister Swede chuckled. "I won't be so flagrant to ask how you managed that." He stuck his hand in a red, white and blue striped bag, then pulled out a hot peanut. He cracked the shell, held the morsel in the palm of his hand, and pontificated, "George Washington Carver took the lowly goober and elevated it to a place of prominence. That's exactly what you're doing by donating to the suffrage movement. One day your lowly voice will be heard in the voting booth." With that, the peanut disappeared into Mister Swede's open mouth. He cracked another peanut, and asked, "By the way, Olivia, where did you send the money this year?"

"I mailed a check to Carrie Chapman Catt. She's the new president of the women's suffrage movement. Along with the money, I wrote a letter, telling Miss Catt that I firmly believe the chances of women gaining the right to vote are definitely improving."

"Missus Catt may be making gains in certain states, but her overall strategy to marginalize minorities in the process leaves me cold. She calls the noble Plains Indians "murderous Sioux", and demands that immigrants be stripped of their right to vote. That woman even declared white supremacy will be strengthened by women's suffrage. Now I ask you, is that someone you want to support?" I didn't have a come-back for Mister Swede. I sat in silence and stared straight ahead. "I'm afraid, Olivia, that a woman's right to vote might not come in our lifetime."

"Why?" I asked. The question made me feel like a ten-year-old Olivia. I searched Mister Swede's eyes for an answer.

"America will soon be entangled in the war going on in

Europe. Only men will go to fight and die, therefore only men will be allowed the right to vote."

"But President Wilson swore we would never go 'over there'."

"Mister Wilson is a politician and will say anything to suit the occasion. It's becoming more obvious with the latest newspaper articles that this country is inching closer and closer to declaring war on Germany."

"This country must have better sense than to send American boys to be killed. Those countries in Europe have been at each other's throats for hundreds of years. At least that's what you taught me in World History. I say, unless Heinie steps foot on U.S. soil, what business is it of ours, what happens over in Europe?"

There was a sadness in his watery eyes when Mister Swede said, "America is becoming an empire, Olivia. This country has extended Manifest Destiny from sea to shining sea. If we want to claim another New World for the Empire, then we'll have to extend our search outside the North American continent."

Our conversation was cut short when from the baseball field, the umpire called out, "Play ball."

****

On April 2, 1917, the day the Greenwood Black Sox started their spring training President Wilson declared war on Germany. War fever raged throughout the Tulsa white community and Negro Wall Street as well. One day, as Alicia and I were strolling down Greenwood Avenue, she pointed to a sign hanging in a store window.

"Mama," she asked. "Who is that old man with the white goatee and the top hat?"

"That's Uncle Sam," I replied.

"My Uncle Sam? But he's white."

"Alicia, that man is everybody's Uncle Sam. Well, everybody whose an American citizen."

"Why does he want me?"

I stopped walking and looked down at my daughter, who was slowly turning into a young lady, one with a million questions just like her mother when she was young. "Sweet One, Uncle Sam doesn't want you. He wants fighting men to go over there."

Alicia stared up at me, and asked, "Oh, you mean like

Daddy, right?"

****

That evening, we gathered around Mama's kitchen table to celebrate Jerome's twenty-first birthday. Mama Rose had baked her son his favorite dessert, a lemon bundt cake. I could tell it did Mama good to watch Jerome, James and Alicia stuff cake down their guts like growing children. It seemed my hormones had decided to tell my fat cells to grow larger. I nibbled on cake crumbs while sipping green herbal tea.

Jerome tapped the side of his empty plate with a fork. When he had everyone's attention, without a hint of emotion, my brother announced, "I've gone and joined the Army."

"You what?" The immediate shocked response came from all of us at the same time.

"Why, Jerome?" Mama pleaded. "Why in the world did you go and do something like that?"

"Because Mama. It's every young man's duty to enlist in the service of his country. Especially men of the Negro variety."

"I buy Liberty Bonds," Mama said. "That should be enough to support the troops."

"Mama's right." I looked at my crazy brother and wondered if he had taken a blow to the head or was just plain dumb. "You don't have to join the army, Jerome. It's voluntary. Now, maybe if a Negro had the right to vote – then I'd say we all owe it to our country to enlist. But until the white's treat Negros as equals, as far as I'm concerned, it's a white man's war."

James vigorously shook his head. "I disagree, Olivia. Negros fought valiantly alongside white men during the war between the states. There wasn't a coward or traitor among them. Now, we're being called upon again, in the defense of this nation. What choice do we have?"

"Hogwash," Mama blurted. "The Negros back then were fighting for their freedom. Today, the Hun is over there not over here. If he does land on our shores, then we'll push him back to where he came from and be done with it. My advice is, don't go looking for a fight somewhere else, you might find one."

Jerome got to his feet, poured fresh coffee into a cup and added one sugar cube. My only misguided brother stirred the steamy liquid, and declared, "There have been Negros fighting over in France since nineteen-fourteen. Some of those men have come back home and have enlisted in the U. S. Army. I say if they're prepared to sacrifice their lives in the name of liberty, justice and the American way, then by God, so am I."

I sat stone-still in my chair imagining Jerome waving the American flag while playing Yankee Doodle Dandy on his clarinet. Then James rose to his feet and walked over to stand next to Jerome. Although my husband was a couple of inches taller and the shade of his skin darker, the two handsome men looked like they could have been brothers.

My dear husband looked directly at Mama. "Since I've been a part of this family your son has been like a brother to me. And what do brothers do? They stick together, right?" The silence in the kitchen was deafening as James turned to look at me. "I'll join the army with Jerome. Together, we'll be cogs in the great machinery of war. We'll fight in obscurity and return to our loved-ones as conquering heroes, God willing, sound in mind and body."

It was a good thing I was young and could still take a shock to my system. My chin dropped to my chest with a 'thud'. I felt woozy and had to grab Mama's arm to stay upright in my chair.

CHAPTER NINETEEN
I WANT YOU

On the same evening my husband dropped the bombshell that he was enlisting in the army with Jerome, I lay awake in bed with my eyes wide open, staring at the dark water stain, starting to form in one corner of the ceiling. I could see a man's face trying to emerge from the brown puffy spots, but when James crawled into bed, I rolled over to face the wall, taking all the covers with me. James muttered, "Damn hormones," and turned off the light.

The next morning, James and I were in the kitchen. He was sitting at the table pretending to read the morning newspaper. I stood holding the coffee pot in one hand, silently staring at the top of my man's hard head. I couldn't keep my emotions or my mouth in check a moment longer.

He looked up, gave me a crooked half smile, and asked, "What's the matter, Sugar? You got any more of that delicious chicory coffee, which I've truly learned to love?"

I set the pot on the table without pouring a drop in James' empty cup. "Why are you doing this to me?"

"I'm joining the Army because I love you, Olivia."

"What?" I screeched. "You can't be serious."

"Baby, we can't have Jerome going over there and not coming back home, can we? It would kill your Mama and you, too. If I enlist and go with him, then we watch each other's back. We'll be like a fighting army of two brothers, Negro brothers at that."

I sighed and flopped down on the chair next to James.

"I'm through arguing about this. What about Alicia? Have you thought how your decision might affect your daughter?"

"Before I leave, I'll make sure she understands what's going on. Besides, Alicia will have you and Mama Rose. When someone asks her, 'What did your daddy do in the war?', you want her to be proud of me, don't you?"

I was not the least bit interested in how Alicia would respond to such a silly question, and I sure wasn't convinced of James' cockeyed idea of keeping Jerome out of harm's way. As a matter of fact, I thought the idea would get both men killed.

"You know, James, I don't complain when you're gone for weeks at a time with the Black Sox, do I?" He shrugged. "And I don't give you grief when you come home and spend two or three evenings a week at Willard's Billiard Parlor. But if you go through with this, I don't know if I can ever forgive you. I didn't marry you to wind up a widow with a child before I turned thirty."

James took me in his arms and whispered, "I know, I know, Sugar. Look, you know I wouldn't be doing this if it wasn't for Jerome. I've come to grow fond of the guy." He gently pushed me back where he could look into my eyes. "Besides, he's my brother, too."

"But who'll manage the baseball team if you're not here?"

James shrugged. "I've already lost my first baseman and two outfielders to the war. Mister Stradford said the team will go into hiatus until this whole fighting thing blows over." He rose from his chair and planted a kiss on my forehead. Holding me by the shoulders, James looked into my eyes. "It's this way, Sweetheart. After Jerome and I enlist they'll send us someplace in Iowa for training. By the time we're soldiers, the war will be over, and we'll be back home safe and sound, okay?"

I whispered, "Okay."

My female intuition, or maybe it was my hormones, told me that it wasn't okay. If James went over there, he might come back and he might not, but if he did return, I just knew that my husband would not be the same man he was before he left.

****

The morning after Mama and I bid James and Jerome a teary farewell at the Frisco train station, we returned home. All day long I walked around despondent and ill at ease with a pain in my heart. By late afternoon the terrible ache had eased somewhat, and I was on the hunt for my daughter.

"Alicia. Alicia. Where is that girl?"

It was not like her to disappear without telling me, but now Alicia was nowhere to be found. After a fruitless search of the house, I hurried across the street and eventually found myself standing on the back porch of Mama's house, staring at the lilac tree in the distance.

"I wonder..." I muttered to myself, stepping off the porch. I headed toward the old outhouse that still stood next to the lilac tree. "Alicia. Are you in there?" There was no answer. I knelt down on all fours and spread the lower branches apart. "Alicia, I'm coming in."

A soft voice, whispered, "Okay, Mama."

"Ow." A sharp branch scraped the side of my arm, but I kept crawling until I was face to face with Alicia. "What are you still doing in here? You know perfectly well it's time for your Spanish lesson. What will Professor Swede think if you're late?"

There was a moment of stony silence, then Alicia hissed, "I don't care what Professor Swede thinks. He can give me all the demerits he wants."

I sat cross-legged on an old saddle blanket, surrounded by pieces of broken pottery and pinecones hanging like Christmas ornaments from the branches. Except for the fact that I was a few pounds heavier, several years older and six inches taller, it was almost like I was back in my own little nest in Missouri.

Pointing to the brown and white striped saddle blanket, I looked at Alicia, and asked, "Do you know where this came from?"

"Missouri. Mama Rose already told me. She said it used to be your security blanket on the wagon train."

"Mama Rose is one-hundred-percent right." I pointed to a framed photograph sitting on a little child's table. "Oh, Alicia, isn't that sweet. It's your Daddy and me on our wedding day." I looked at my daughter and had to smile. "Alicia, I can't believe you did all of this?" She shrugged. "I didn't know you were so creative."

"That's because you're never around. You're always at the grocery store, with Grandma Rose or Banana John. And now..."

Alicia clammed up. Tears welled up in her eyes and rolled down her cheeks. I put my arm around her shoulder and scooted closer.

"And now?" I asked.

It took her a few moments but finally she found the words. "Now Daddy's gone, too. Why did he have to go over there? When is he coming back home?"

"Your Daddy will be back before you know it. He wants to make sure Uncle Jerome stays safe and comes back home, too. This country is at war. It's up to everyone to pitch in and do their share."

Alicia sniffed a couple of times and wiped her nose with my hanky. "I can help, too. I'm old enough."

"Of course, you can. Now, will you come out of here, so Professor Swede won't be mad. You know how upset he gets when we're late."

"Okay, Mama." Alicia clutched her store-bought Colored baby-doll with the two long black horsehair braids that had replaced Ree Ree, the poor thing had disintegrated into rags and was buried next to the lilac tree. Before making a move to leave, Alicia looked at me and the words rushed out all in one breath. "Mister Banana John says Sicilian lemons make the best lemonade, how 'bout I open a lemonade stand?"

I took a good look at my daughter and was surprised how much she looked like Mama Rose. The copper-brown color of her hair was a shade lighter than the brown color of her skin. Alicia was also blessed with Mama's generous mouth and full lips.

"Yes, Dear," I sighed, "you can open a lemonade stand."

****

It was sweltering hot that day in August, when I stepped inside the Greenwood Post Office. James and Jerome had been gone for over two months and there had been no word from either one. Hoping for news from the frontlines, I held my breath and opened the bronze door to our mailbox.

"Nothing but bills," I grumbled, riffling through the pile of envelopes. Then, I came to the one with the postmark, Des Moines, Iowa. I finally exhaled and held the thin missive over my chest. Clutching the daily mail in one hand and the single envelope in the other, I hurried directly home where I placed a kettle half full of water on the stove to boil.

I squeezed the juice of a Sicilian lemon into a blue Wedgewood teacup while reciting one of my favorite poems. 'Till, his best step approaching, We journey to the Day, And tell each other how We sung To Keep the Dark away'

When the water reached the boiling point, I made a cup of Earl Gray tea and took a seat at the table. While waiting for the tea to cool, I traced the curved letters on the front of the envelope with the tip of my finger. The postmark was dated July fifteenth. It had taken over three weeks for James's letter to arrive in Greenwood. I wondered if my husband was still in Iowa, or if he and Jerome had already been sent over there. I picked up the sterling silver knife that rested on the sterling silver butter dish and was just about ready to slit open the envelope, when I heard the front door open and close. I turned to see Mama coming toward the kitchen. She made a groaning sound when she took the seat next to me and started thumbing through the stack of daily mail.

"Nothing but bills," she grumbled.

"Uh-huh," I mumbled in agreement, and held up the letter from James.

Mama leaned forward and squinted. Once she was able to focus and read the name, she settled back in her chair. "You haven't opened it yet?"

When the letter was laying on the table, I read the first page to myself, then turned toward Mama.

"James says that he and Jerome made it to camp safely, but the white men in charge of the training refuse to teach them how to use some of the weapons."

"Why that sounds ridiculous." Mama shook her head and clicked her tongue in a scolding manner. "If they're not going to let the men defend themselves, why did they let them join-up?"

I shrugged and kept reading. "He writes that Negros are only allowed to do menial jobs."

Mama thought for a moment, the put on a big smile, "Good. I'm glad they
won't let James and Jerome shoot guns. Instead of living in the trenches, our two
boys will peel potatoes behind the front lines. That sounds safe."

I turned to the second page and read further, then laughed out loud. "James says not to worry about Jerome. When the officers found out he could play the clarinet, they put him in the company band. The only marching he'll do is in victory parades."

"What about James? Does he say where he's being sent?"

I read the last lines on the third page out loud, "I've been assigned to the Three-hundred-sixty-ninth Division. We leave in a week or two, but don't worry. From what I hear the war is almost over. By the time I get to France the only thing they'll want me to do is march under the Arc de Triomphe'. I love you Olivia, and Alicia. I miss you both terribly. Tell everyone back home I miss them, too."

CHAPTER TWENTY
OFFER REFUSED

My husband's prediction of a quick ending to the hostilities raging in Europe were premature. Without any further letters from James, the trench warfare drug on, until March of 1918. That's when I received a letter that was dated January of that year. The four water-stained pages had been written after James landed in France. His complaints about the food and boredom were to be expected, but the lack of respect he and his fellow Negro enlistees received from the white soldiers, including the officers made me wonder if the American Constitution only applied to white folks.

In another one of his letters, James wrote, "The relations between the French soldiers and their American Negro counterparts is generally good. I often see the French officers and soldiers befriending the Colored troops. They call us "brothers in arms" and treat us with all the courtesy that could be expected in such a trying situation". I refolded the letter, thinking that although my husband was fighting in a war thousands of miles away from Oklahoma, his family still had food to eat, clothes to cover their backs and a roof overhead.

****

Early one morning before the grocery store was open for business, I was helping Mama take inventory when from behind the counter, my dear mother shouted, "Olivia, don't forget to count the canned goods on aisle four."

"Yes, Mama. Thanks for reminding me, for the hundredth

time."

"Olivia, don't expect to walk the primrose path the rest of your life. If there's work to do, we're the ones who have to do it."

"I know, I know, Mama. I'm sorry for the snarky answer. It must be my hormones, again."

"Hormones?"

"Mama, I've told you about those, remember? They're the tiny particles inside a woman's bloodstream that infect her glands." Nothing more came from Mama, so I continued. "Those little boogers are why I can't keep my lips zipped." I leaned over the counter and looked down at the back of Mama's head. "I am truly thankful for all the material wealth and the many blessings that have been bestowed on our family. Nobody, Negro or White can ever claim that the Trulucks or the Binghams are 'Nothin' but lazy niggers'. We work hard, put in long hours and don't grumble, at least not much."

Once my verbal fusillade was over, I went back to diligently restocking canned peas and green bean on aisle four. That's when I heard someone rattle the front door. I raised my head to see two Negros standing outside. I rapped on the glass with my knuckles and shook my head.

"We're not open." I pointed at the sign hanging on the door that clearly indicated our hours of operation. "Come back in an hour."

The smaller of the two was hatless with a clean-shaven face, cropped hair and pageboy bangs. Dressed in a form-fitting tailor-made gray flannel suit with a black ribbon bowtie tied tight around his neck the strange looking creature kept rapping the brass handle against the door. He was insistent on gaining entrance.

"Dang salesmen," I grumbled, and shook my head "no", again.

"Open up." The belligerent individual pressed his nose against the glass that left a smudge streak. "It's very important to your business."

The large man who stood behind the shorter individual, popped open a paper bag then, like he was a starving animal, started stuffing handfuls of the thick greasy potato chips in his open maw.

From the back of the store, Mama called out, "Who is it, Olivia?"

"I'm not sure, Mama. They're either salesmen or two well-dressed hobos."

"What are they selling?"

I unlocked the door and immediately came face to face with the short one. "May I help you?"

"The question is, Missy. Can we help you?"

The short one nodded and extended a right hand. "The moniker's Pat." When we shook hands, I was surprised that Pat's hand was as soft as silk. I felt a tinge of jealousy when I noticed his well-manicured, long, shiny fingernails. Nodding toward the giant accomplice, Pat said, "My friend's name is Munchie."

Munchie grunted, which I assumed was the full extent of his vocabulary. Instead of looking at me, his full attention was on the tiny pies Mama had baked that morning.

Mama had ventured to the front of the store. With hands on her hips, she gave the well-dressed fancy dudes a one-eyed up-and-down stare. "What are you two smarters selling that we don't already have?" Mama's usually pleasant voice had been replaced by a sharp irritated rasp.

Pat stood on tiptoes, shaking his forefinger right in Mama's face. "Think of us as insurance salesmen. Munchie and I will give you something to stand under when it's raining, get my drift?"

Mama bent over at the waist to shove her nose in the little guy's face. "We don't need any of your insurance, you got that, Mister Pat?"

"Maybe you might want to reconsider," Pat said, with a sly chuckle. "If you're smart, you'll go along with the rest of your wang-dang-doodle neighbors. You get that, sister?"

The lines in Mama's forehead had deepened. "Listen here, Buster Brown, I'm not your sister. I don't care how far up the tree of man you go. You and me? We ain't related. Now, I got work to do. You and your gorilla take a hike."

Pat kept an eye on Mama as he back-peddled out the door and kept yakking, "That kind of talk will get you rained on. We'll give you time to think about it, but I'm warnin' you, don't take too long. This is a one-time offer – it's up to you what happens next."

Munchie nodded toward the shelf that held Mama's baked goods. He removed his derby, to look sideways at her and asked, "If it ain't too much trouble Ma'am, can I buy me a dozen of them tiny pies, please?"

****

Armistice was declared in November 1918, but there was still no word from James. Thanksgiving along with Christmas came and went. In February 1919, I read in the Greenwood Gazette that the Three-hundred-and-sixty-ninth Division had returned from overseas. Its soldiers had been honored in a parade under a blizzard of ticker tape. It was also observed in the Gazette that after proudly marching down Fifth Avenue in New York City the very same men, who put their lives on the line defending freedom, were denied service at the Whites-Only saloons, hotels and restaurants.

One month after the gala celebration, held in honor of this country's brave Negro soldiers, a Model T chugged to a stop in front of our house. There was a loud blast from the car's horn. I was busy in the kitchen, washing dishes. I figured it was probably Jerome. He had a way of announcing his arrival with an 'A-hoo-ga, a-hoo-ga'. I was still scrubbing at the burned, blackened baked cheese residue on one of my blue enamel cooking pots, when I heard a loud banging on the front door.

I wiped my wet hands on a dish towel, shouting, "Who is it?"

When I was halfway down the hallway my heart started beating triple-time. The handsome man standing at the front entrance was my husband.

"Oh, my God, it's James."

I rushed to the screen door, flung it open and fell forward, almost in a dead-faint. If James hadn't been standing there to catch me, I would have fallen flat on my face. For a brief second, the weight of my body pushing against his seemed to make my husband go off-balance, but he quickly regained his equilibrium. I could feel from the way he held me that something wasn't exactly right. Finally, James pulled away to press his lips against mine. We savored a long deep kiss. When we parted, I saw that my husband's right sleeve was folded up and pinned to the shoulder of his shirt.

"James," I gasped. "What happened?"

My wounded warrior gave me a crooked smile and shrugged his left shoulder. "I wanted to make sure the Hun didn't forget the Three-sixty-ninth so I left him a little memento to remember us by."

****

The following weekend our entire family gathered at Mama Rose's house. After a bounteous meal of roasted pheasant, creamed asparagus, boiled potatoes and cinnamon apples, Jerome leaned back in his chair to rub his full belly, then fired-up one of Banana John's gifted Dutch Master stinky cigars.

Jerome exhaled a white cloud of smoke and chuckled. "Uncle Sam kept me real busy, Mama. The U. S. Army's All-Negro Band played at bond rallies all over the country. Once the collection plate had been passed around, it was on to the next town. We didn't get much shut-eye, the food was lousy bow-wow mutton, and we had sadistic tyrants for officers."

"You poor baby," Mama said, and gently patted Jerome's shoulder. "You were not cut out for the army life. But now that you and James are home safe and sound, everything will be just fine."

Professor Swede, who tended to nod-off during late evening meals, was still conscious enough to contribute his two-cents worth. The old tutor scratched his head and looked around the table. When his eyes landed on my brother, Mister Swede cleared his throat, and pronounced, "Yes, yes, Jerome, everyone knows you served your country honorably." Next, he turned to my husband. "And where exactly was it that you lost your arm, James?"

Since his return home, I'd noticed that James was uncomfortable talking about his wartime experiences. Before I could change the subject, my husband came up with the answer.

"It was during the Meuse-Argonne offensive. We fought the Hun from September, all the way up to the Armistice. Forty-seven days we lived in those rank trenches, wallowing in our own filth. It was a month of pure, unmitigated hell. The Three-sixty-ninth lost over one-hundred men."

Mama scooted her chair up next to the stove and shivered. "My-oh-my, that must've been terrible"

"That's right, Mama," Jerome said. "I heard-tell that if the doughboys weren't mowed down by the German machine-gunners, the Spanish flu would finish them off."

James nodded. "The Hun wasn't immune to the plague, either."

My voice was a whisper when I spoke. "Not only were the

poor men dying from bullets they had to fight an even more deadly enemy from within. A germ doesn't choose sides." I pulled a hairbrush from my apron and started to comb Alicia's shoulder length hair, which was straight as an arrow and thick as fescue grass. "The Spanish pest attacked Greenwood last year. We've lost twenty souls that I know of. I've never been to so many funerals. I wear a surgical mask in the grocery store. They say it keeps the bug at bay."

Mama looked tired as she nodded in agreement. "It seems like all I've been doin' is tending to the sick and the dying."

"That plus replacing broken windows and stomping out trash fires," I muttered.

"That's the first I've heard about all that," Jerome and James both said.

Mama just sat studying her coffee cup, while I filled-in the two with the details. "Two thugs are trying to extort Mama. They've been breaking windows and setting fire to the trash. Sometimes they come inside the store. They don't buy anything, just stand around picking up stuff then setting it down someplace else. They make the other customers feel uncomfortable."

"Munchie does buy all my tiny pies," Mama offered.

"They want Mama to pay them protection money, but she refuses. They haven't resorted to any physical violence, yet. One is a smallish fellow but the other one, he's a big Goliath."

"Are these men white or Negro?" James asked.

"Negros," I said.

"What the hell," Jerome barked. "We're gonna' have to do something about those two ruffians."

Mama reached over and patted Jerome's hand. "Son, you just got back from a war. Why look for more trouble? We got enough on our plate right now dealing with that flu bug." Mama scooted her chair closer to Jerome and put her hand on his forehead then felt his chubby cheeks. "You feel warm. Stay with me for a few days and let me take care of you."

"Mama, I've been sitting by the stove. I'm bound to feel hot to the touch. Don't go frettin' about me. It's you I worry about. We can't have some two-bit punks trashing Rose's Grocery, right James?"

"You got that right, Jerome."

While Mama and I cleared the table, I caught snatches of

the men's conversation and overheard James whisper, "We'll teach those two goons a lesson they won't forget."

Jerome tugged on James's empty shirt sleeve. "Let's flip a coin to see who gets the big one."

CHAPTER TWENTY-ONE
A FRIEND INDEED

I stood next to James as he sat on the edge of Alicia's bed. Our daughter looked up and searched her father's eyes. "You're never going to go to war again, right Daddy?"

"That's right," James said, tucking the patchwork quilt under Alicia's chin.

"And those Spanish flu germs that Granma Rose talked about. They won't get us either, will they Daddy?"

"You're absolutely right again. No, they won't," James said, shaking his head from side to side.

As James continued to console our daughter's fears, I was still mulling over what I'd overheard earlier that evening between him and Jerome. By this time I was fit to be tied, so I retired to my bedroom to wait. When James tiptoed inside, I was sitting ramrod straight in bed with my arms folded across my chest. My dear husband stood next to the bed, looking at me while wearing a big smile.

"Why the puffed-out lower lip, Sugar Dumplin'?"

I glared and asked, "James, you're not really serious about this, are you?"

"About what?"

He walked around to his side of the bed while removing his shirt exposing a raw-looking stump where his arm should have been.

"James," I said, having a hard time keeping the tone of my

voice under control. "Have you considered that when you and Jerome confront those two lawless niggers, there'll be a fight. They have guns. I know because I've seen them when they come into the store. The small one always makes sure his jacket is hanging wide open." I stopped to catch my breath, then continued, "I just heard you tell Alicia that you'd never go to war, again. What do you call picking a fight with two thugs? a picnic? Please James," I begged. "Don't go looking for trouble."

"Baby, we're just gonna' have a bear meeting with those two. What's their names, again?"

"Pat and Munchie."

"Are nothing but cheap, two-bit punks tryin' to shake down honest business owners. Jerome and I intend to put an end to it."

James sunk down on the edge of the bed. I scooted further toward my side. "Well," I huffed, "I'm going with you."

James chuckled and craned his neck to look at me. "No, you're not. We don't want to take a chance of messin' up this beautiful face, do we?"

I turned my back on my husband. "I'm going."

"Now, Olivia, you are not getting involved in this and that's a direct order."

I turned to look James square in his eyes. "Oh, really? And who promoted you to Commander in Chief?"

"Listen, Olivia…all I'm tryin' to…"

"All you're trying to do is control me. In case you haven't noticed, Mister James Monroe Bingham, while you've been gone, I've been the straw boss around here. Besides, you only have one arm. And Jerome? Why that twerp is just a kid who's never been in a real fight in his life, except with me, and I always beat the tar out of him."

There was hurt in James' eyes, and I immediately regretted opening my big mouth. He reached over and took my hand in his. "Olivia, this has to be settled man to man. It's been going on long enough. We both know, I can't go to the police. Those white wise-ass cracker cops in Tulsa would laugh in my face. It's written in the Greenwood charter, conflicts between citizens have to be settled amongst themselves…hopefully peacefully."

"Well, I'm going," I countered, pulled the quilt up to my chin and closed my eyes like I was asleep.

"Okay, Baby Cakes, suit yourself," James huffed. "I'll sleep on the sofa."

He stalked out of the bedroom and for first time since we'd been married, I fell asleep that night without telling my husband, "I love you".

****

Early the next morning, I was sitting in the cramped office of Rose's Grocery #2. I was there to pick up the previous day's cash receipts. "I can't believe it," I said, while flipping through a stack of paper currency. "Number Two's sales have grown by leaps and bounds. The deposit will be almost as much as Mama Rose's."

Banana John wallowed the ever-present unlit Dutch Master cigar stuck in the corner of his mouth, then leaned over to shoot a stream of black tobacco juice into the spittoon. "It ain't hard to do good business when you got good products." There was a hint of pinkish embarrassment on his cheeks, when Banana John looked at me. "And because of you, I can add and subtract. That's why I'm the boss here."

"And a good one, too," I admitted.

Banana John kept his eyes glued on mine, and asked, "What's the matter wit' you, Olivia? You're talkin' about-a good things but your words they sound sad. Something...somebody bothering you?"

I shrugged, broke off the staring contest, and dropped a wad of greenbacks into my leather pouch. "Banana John, you must be a wrinkle reader. It's nothing. I'm just tired."

"You're too young to be just tired. Look at me. You got a' old man sittin' here who's got-a the nose that can smell when somethin's rotten' in Denmark."

When the light hit Banana John just right, to me it looked as if a wispy halo hovered over his head. My best white friend, not counting Professor Swede, kept his crinkled, wizened eyes glued on me until I finally spilled my guts.

"I am terribly worried. When James was gone, Mama and I have been repeatedly terrorized."

"Pat and Munchie," Banana John mumbled.

"Yes, but, how did..."

"Couple of months ago those two come-a in here. I tell them, go to hell and kiss-a my ass. They don't come-a back. Olivia, why don't you tell me sooner about this?"

"Because…oh, I don't know. Maybe I thought that sooner or later they'd just go away. At 9:00 a.m. tomorrow, James and Jerome are going to Willard's Billiard Parlor. They're going to have a bear meeting with Pat and Munchie." At that point I started sniffing and had to wipe my eyes with a handkerchief, before asking, "Is there anything you can do, Banana John? Please, talk to James. Tell him not to go. Maybe he'll listen to another man."

Banana John removed the soggy stogie from between his lips, lowered his chin, let loose a stream of black saliva into the spittoon. Then, he looked at me, wiped his mouth with the back of his hand, and said, "I'm-a sorry, Olivia. Banana John can't stick-a his nose into another man's business."

"I wasn't implying that you step in, directly." Then, I had an idea. "Banana John, I've heard that you have…certain friends. Maybe if you dropped a hint, they could take care of the problem for me."

Banana John nodded. "Maybe they can, maybe they can't. But if-a they do, they come with a hefty price tag."

"Name it."

"You pay nothing. I do it for-a Mama Rose, she make-a Banana John a rich man."

****

The next morning, I trailed behind James and Jerome as we marched down Greenwood Avenue, headed toward Willard's Billiard Parlor. Once we were inside the dark, smelly joint the three of us stood with our mouths wide open. It looked as if someone had beat us to the punch. Munchie was laying on the floor in a corner, curled up in a fetal position. When I was standing over the big man, he turned his head and looked up at me. His face was covered with blood and his nose had been moved at least a half-inch to the left. With one eye swollen shut, Munchie opened his good one and held his hands up in front of his face.

"No, more," Munchie begged. "Please, don't hit me no more."

I turned toward James, and asked, "What have they done with the other one?"

"Who's they?" he asked.

"In here," Jerome called out.

I saved my answer to James's question for a later time. When the three of us were inside the poolhall's office, James

135

chuckled. "Well, well, well. Would ya' look at that wall hanging."

The collar of Pat's coat had been snagged on a wall-hook, leaving the tips of the short man's toes barely skimming the floor. "Get me down from here," Pat screeched, wildly wiggling. "Get me down from here or I'll...I'll..."

"Or you'll what?" Jerome took a step toward the thrashing thug. Like a boxer trying for a K.O., with his fists tightly clenched, Pat flailed empty air. "Careful there, sonny," Jerome teased, "or you might strain something."

James said, "I think he should stay there until we decide what to do with him."

"Oh, James," I said, "let the poor man down."

"Think so?" James asked, his voice all smarmy. "Say, Olivia, you wouldn't happen to know who might have done this, do you?"

I looked up at the low hanging ceiling, and replied, "It must have been friends of a friend."

CHAPTER TWENTY-TWO
THE RED SCARE

It was late-April 1919. Spring had blossomed, filling the balmy air with the sweet, heady fragrance of flowers. "A perfect day to be outside," I decided, and went looking for James. I found my husband sitting alone in the darkened parlor, vacantly staring out the window. I tiptoed across the room and quietly took a seat next to him on the camel-back sofa. Outside the window, on our front lawn two neighbor boys were throwing a baseball back and forth.

"Maybe you could go out there and show them how to throw a curve ball."

He gave me a defeated look and shook his head. "Olivia, I'm not a southpaw."

I leaned closer to the man I loved dearly and rested my head on his shoulder. "Do you remember when you showed me how to make the ball do the dipsy-doodle?"

"I do. It was late at night. We were in your parents' backyard."

"It was so dark I didn't see it coming."

"It came like this." James leaned over to kiss my lips.

"Yes," I whispered, then kissed him long and hard.

When the smooching was over, he looked at me, frowning. "This year the Black Sox are hiring a new manager. You do realize my baseball playing days are over, right? I could go back to the oil fields, but I'd have to take a cut in pay as a "lumper". When James looked at me, his sad eyes told me how much he was hurting inside. "I know you're tired of hearing all this, so I'll shut up."

I'd been tiptoeing around what had become the big road

apple in the punchbowl of our happy marriage. Right then and there, I said, "James, let's clear the air. You're not any less of a man now than when you left Greenwood. I still love you, no matter if you have one arm or four of them. Mama always said, "Life is like a grindstone, whether it whittles you down or polishes you up depends on the stuff you're made of"."

James wrapped his arm around my shoulder, pulled me close and tight, almost squeezing me breathless. "Do you think there's a pearl hidden inside this old oyster shell?"

"Of course, there is. Black pearls are far rarer than white ones."

"You're still my rare gem, and a joy to live with."

****

It started with a fever. Everybody in the family hoped it would go away. After hundreds of prayers and gallons of chicken soup, her temperature shot up to 102.5. Along with the fever there was vomiting and diarrhea. It only took one week for a normal healthy, one-hundred-fifty-pound woman to shrink down to a ninety-pound skeleton covered in a skin-suit. The Spanish flu had come to Greenwood and was parked in Mama Truluck's living room. James and I were in her kitchen. I stood by the stove, wiping my eyes with the tail end of an apron. He sat at the table, staring at the calendar hanging on the opposite wall.

"Mama's not getting any better," I said, fighting back tears that were building up.

"Did you see the dark spots on her cheeks?" James asked, his voice flat and emotionless.

I shrugged my weary shoulders and shook my head. "They're all over her body. Doctor Jackson says it's from internal bleeding that won't stop."

James eyes finally turned his head to focus on me. "She keeps asking about Sodom and Gomorrah."

"That's what Brother Sin-Eater called Joplin, Missouri. Mama must be back in that old hay wagon, going West. Good Lord, but that was a brutal trip."

Then from the living room, we heard Mama's weak voice, "Olivia. Olivia."

When James and I were standing next to the sofa, Mama looked up at me and tried to force a smile. "Olivia, do you remember when we left Missouri?"

"I do, Mama," I said, taking her limp hand in mine. "I think about that often."

"Do you remember when I told you not to look back?"

For a moment I was stumped, because I spent most of the cross-country trip to Oklahoma sitting in the rear of the wagon, looking back at where we'd been. But in the interest of placating a dying woman, I agreed, "Yes, Mama. I remember that quite well."

"Good, good," Mama whispered, taking my hand and gently squeezing my fingers. "Look not behind thee, God said. But Lot's wife, she didn't heed His word."

"Mama," I said, "you've got no regrets to look back on. You always did the right thing. At no time did you harm another soul, either by word or deed."

"Pillar of salt," Mama mumbled, "pillar of salt."

"I'll stay with her," I said, turning to James. "You go on, get some rest."

James left to get Alicia ready for school that day, then he would open the grocery store. My husband and I had decided that in the best interest of his mental health and the future financial success of Rose's Grocery Store, James would step in and shoulder part of the everyday burden of running a thriving business.

By late afternoon, Mama's breathing had become labored. No matter how hard I pounded on her back, nothing worked to get the necessary oxygen into her lungs. She had trouble catching her breath, then I noticed her skin was turning blue.

"Okay, Mama, okay," I whispered, gently letting her head rest on the pillow. "If it's your time, it's your time. I won't prolong your agony."

Mama's eyes were wide open when she coughed. A pink frothy substance trickled from the corner of her mouth. I watched as the life-force oozed from her body, to be absorbed back into the cosmos.

After closing Mama's eyelids, I kissed her cheek and whispered, "Goodbye, Mama. I love you. We all love you so very much."

****

During Mama's wake, it's quite possible that most of the citizens of Greenwood passed through her parlor. Copious amounts of tears were shed, and sincere condolences were freely given. Mama's earthly remains were nestled in the one-hundred-percent, guaranteed-not-to-leak-until-Jesus-returned, coffin that Daddy had built years earlier. After she was laid-low, friends cleaned up the mess left behind by the mourners, while I sat on the back porch. There was a breeze blowing from the south. For some reason I couldn't sit still. So, I got up and strolled toward the thriving lilac tree I'd planted by the old outhouse so many years ago.

When I was standing next to the tree, from inside, Alicia asked, "Mama?"

"Yes, Dear. Can I come in?"

"Uh-huh."

After worming my way through the green boughs, I sat cross-legged next to my beautiful Alicia. Averting her eyes, she wouldn't look up at me, until I asked, "Are you okay?" She finally rolled her tear-filled eyes in my direction with a silent shrug. I scooted closer and wiped her wet cheeks with a hanky. "You know, Alicia, Mama Rose wouldn't want you to be so sad. Don't you remember what your grandma always said?" Alicia shrugged, again but this time, with a soft sigh. "A woman who lives life fully is prepared to die at any time."

Alicia sniffed a couple of times and gave me a squinty one-eyed look. "Mama Rose didn't say that."

"I know, Dear," I said, brushing wisps of Alicia's coal black curly hair from her forehead. "But if Mark Twain hadn't, your Mama Rose surely would've."

I noticed that Alicia's little girl features were changing. Now, she was starting to look more and more like Mama Rose. She had Mama's same chin and her eyes were big and round, not almond shaped like mine. Although, her rather sharp, hawk-like nose and high cheek bones did show a close resemblance to my facial features. All in all, my daughter was pleasing to look at, and one day, in the not-too-distant future, she was destined to become a boy magnet.

Alicia studied me with her determined, questioning eyes. Tentatively, she asked, "Mama, why are we here?"

"Well, Dear, I thought I'd already explained how you got here. Remember when I told you how a man and woman..."

"No, Mama. I'm not talking about the birds and the bees. I want to know why. Why did God put us here and for such a short time?" Alicia shook her head. "None of it makes any sense to me. None at all."

I took a deep breath and looked up at the lilac branches swaying overhead. "Mama Rose always told me that no matter how much time on Earth we're allotted, the reason we're here is to help one another and be happy."

****

By that autumn, Professor Swede, along with several Negro Army veterans formed the Negro Students for a Socialist Society. The N.S.S.S. held their weekly meetings in the parlor of Mama's house, where Professor Swede had taken up residence. It was one evening when James had taken Alicia to the Dreamland Theater to see Mary Pickford in Daddy-Long-Legs, that I marched across the street to Mama's place. There, I was met on the front porch by a peach fuzz fellow not much older than Alicia. "Yes, Ma'am. Can I help you?"

"No, young man, you may not."

I placed my hand on the doorknob to enter, but he stated, "I'm sorry, Ma'am, but no ladies are allowed inside."

"I beg your pardon? See here, young man, I happen to own this house. So, if you don't mind, please step away from the door or I shall remove you myself."

The fire burning in my eyes must have singed the poor fellow's face. He backed away and stepped aside to allow me to enter. Once I was inside, Mister Swede came limping toward me from the parlor. Behind him was a porty man with a neatly trimmed beard. When the two were standing next to me in the foyer, I shook hands with the stranger.

"Allow me to present Mister James Weldon Johnson," Mister Swede said. "He's our guest speaker tonight."

After a brief exchange of pleasantries, I asked, "Tell me, Mister Johnson, what is your subject matter?"

"The delicate predicament in which the Negro race finds itself. Hundreds of colored people have died this summer. Thousands of others have suffered the most horrible indignities. White supremacists-terrorist attacks have occurred in more than three dozen cities. The worse violence took place in Elaine, Arkansas, where over two-hundred Negros were butchered."

Not to be left out of the conversation, Mister Swede found enough wind in his pipes to contribute. "This has been a 'Red Summer' for the colored race. The country is in an economic slump. Veterans, both Negro and White, have returned and they're all looking for jobs. Only by joining hands and working together can we hope to build a just society that benefits people of all colors."

"There's only one thing the white oligarchs fear and that's solidarity among the workers," Mister Johnson added. "Negro and White. Together we win. Divided we fail."

It suddenly occurred to me that neither man had clearly articulated the real stumbling block sitting in the way of progress, so I let my belief be known. "Although, I believe it's important for all races to work together, the only way Negros will find equality is through the ballot box."

****

Later that evening, when I returned home, I found my husband sitting in our bedroom engrossed in reading the late edition newspaper. I was still so all fired-up from Mister Johnson's speech that I pounded pillows with my fists then threw them at James. I walked around the bed, stood in front of my husband and pulled the pillows off of his lap.

James looked up at me and mouthed the word, "What?"

"Don't you care?" I asked.

"About what?" he asked, the decibel of his voice rising.

"About rampant racism, freedom denied, Negros murdered. Do you need more? There's no reason why Negros in this country should be afraid for our lives. We've already fought the Civil War. The Confederates lost. What's not to understand?"

James let the crumpled newspaper fall on the floor, then took my hand to pull me down on his lap. I could see the love in his eyes. "Olivia," he whispered, "you never fail to amaze me. When other women only think about money and clothes, you take on the monumental weight of the Negro race."

"If only we could help. We have enough money. Why don't we make a donation to the N. double A. C. P.?"

"Sure," he said, and gently kissed my fingertips one at a time. I let him envelope me in his strong arm. "Double the amount you give to the women's suffrage movement."

When we were comfortably situated, I asked, "What have you been reading so intently?"

"While we were fighting over in Europe, the Russians were having a revolution."

"Yes, I know. It turned out well for the Communist."

"Mmmm, not so good for the Tsar, but now the newspaper says the Reds are over here, preaching Bolshevism, anarchism and atheism. People are up in arms looking for a Communist under every bed."

"Well, you can get down on the floor and look for yourself, but I guarantee there are no Communist, Socialists or dust bunnies under any of my beds."

"How about in your bed?" James joked, and rose from his chair.

That all depends," I said. "Is the bunny a Commie?"

James shrugged then wrapped his left arm around my waist, pulling me close. "He's neat and dependable."

"That's all the better," I said, as we both sunk down on the bed.

CHAPTER TWENTY-THREE
FOREWARNING

In January 1919, Congress ratified the 18th Amendment. The new law of the land barred the manufacture, sale or transportation of intoxicating liquors for beverage purposes. Mister Swede lectured, "The prohibitionists have driven a stake through John Barleycorn's heart." As we found out, the intentions might have been good, but the results weren't as advertised. Most Americans ignored the "noble experiment" and flocked to speakeasys where bootleg booze of dubious quality was consumed in vast quantities by thirsty patrons.

A year later, to celebrate Independence Day, 1920, I was wrapping our front porch in red, white and blue bunting when I heard a loud, long 'beeeep'. I turned to see Jerome's head leaning out the open window of a shiny blue automobile. When he stepped out of the car, my brother was wearing a cheesy smile. I ran over to give him a big hug, then stepped back to admire Jerome's newest motorized acquisition.

"This thing must have cost you a fortune."

Jerome chuckled. "Who cares, Sis? I didn't have to pay full price, only a little down and a little a month. The man called them 'time-payments'."

When James and Alicia were standing next to the automobile, my husband ran his hand along the shiny front fender. "Congratulations, Jerome. No more Model T's. You've moved up to a luxury ride."

"That's right," Jerome agreed. "It's the three P's now, Packard, Pierce and Peerless. Silence and comfort, that's what the Packard Car Company advertises. This beauty has twelve cylinders and ninety horsepower. Push the pedal to the floor an' it'll leap a mile a minute…just like the economy's been doing. Gosh, it's too bad Woodrow Wilson can't run for president, again."

"Woodrow Wilson," I said. The words left a bad taste in my mouth. "He's the man who got us involved in a needless conflict." I stared at my brother and shook my head, just like Mama used to do when she was all riled-up about something.

Jerome smiled. "You still on your anti-Wilson soap box, Sis?"

"Don't mind her," James said, putting an arm around my shoulders and pulling me close. "Olivia's been attending Professor Swede's more radical lectures. And, since this is an election year…you-know-who is a mite testy."

I looked up at my husband. "I take it you don't care that we're no longer a government of the majority. Instead, the laws are written by a small group of dominant white males who have all the money." I turned my attention back to Jerome. "And you, buying a car on credit. Why I bet Daddy's rolling over in his leakproof coffin. Did you know, Jerome, that Congress passed laws for the dismissal of schoolteachers who are active members of the Communist Party? If we're not careful this country will one day be taken over by a fascist dictatorship."

"Please, Olivia," James begged, "no more of your hormonal politics, please."

I finally shut my clap-trap and gave James a self-satisfied phony smile that he returned in-kind. Alicia hopped upon the running-board, flung open the roadster's passenger door and climbed up on the seat. Testing the springs by bouncing up and down, she exclaimed, "Wow-za. Uncle Jerome, take me for a ride in the Packard…pl-eeese?"

"Sure, kiddo. But before I do, I've some great news." Jerome turned to look at me and James. "My days on the road are over," he announced.

"That is exciting," I said. "Mama would be so happy to hear you won't be camped out in fleabag hotels getting bit by bedbugs and dining on roadkill."

Jerome pretended to choke himself, and said, "No more possum for me."

"Good Lord, Jerome," I said, putting a hand over my stomach. "Daddy used to talk about eating those greasy things. What do they taste like?"

"Mmmmm, soggy wet trash, with hints of vomit."

After we had a good laugh, James asked, "So, Jerome, what's next?"

"Nothing that's illegal," Jerome said with sigh, watching Alicia exit the Packard and slam the door. "I've a plan that will entertain the masses without the need to sell alcohol, but I'll damn well look the other way if you bring your own."

"That sounds wonderful," I said. "This Prohibition nonsense has everybody down in the dumps. Without booze to ease the pain of living, some folks are gonna' be left out on a limb."

Jerome puffed out his chest and declared, "I'm gonna' give Negro Wall Street a vaudeville theater, one that never closes. As a matter of fact, that's what I'll call it 'Jerome's Never Closes'. I'll have comedians, opera singers, dancers, musical reviews, feats of daring-do and animal acts. The paying customer can walk into my theater at any time of the day or night and be entertained. If only gambling were legal…why I'd…we'd all be millionaires."

I chuckled and shook my head. "Jerome, if people are sitting inside your theater for any length of time, you'll have to feed and water them."

"Ah, dear sister," he said, and came over to put an arm around my shoulder. "I've got big plans to put you in the catering business." Jerome turned toward the Packard and shouted, "Alicia, please do not jump up and down in the rumble seat. It might leak a spring."

****

By January 1, 1921, not only had women won the right to vote but Jerome Alvin Truluck had become known as the Negro Jerome Kern of the Greenwood District. He opened Jerome's Never Closes, featuring, a dazzling display of heterogenous splendor, designed to educate, edify, amaze and uplift. Jerome stood on a box out in front of the theater, put a megaphone to his mouth, and declared, "Step right up, folks, there's something inside for everybody. Bring Mom, bring Grandma and bring the kids to see acts of high-and-low-brow entertainment." Not only did everybody flock to Jerome's Never Closes, the-starving-masses brought their appetite and their hip flasks.

****

The day I turned thirty-one, my hormones were running hotter than a two-dollar pistol on a Saturday night at a horse opera. Oh, there was the occasional pain in my lower back. I suppose that reminded me I was functioning on one kidney. To keep up with the food demand at Jerome's Never Closes, James added a small kitchen to the rear of Rose's Grocery. That's where I was, putting together box lunches when James walked in and kissed the back of my neck.

"James, don't. I'm all sweaty."

"C'mon, Olivia, you can take a break. All work and no--"

"Mean's no food for Jerome's hungry mob."

I felt James' hands on my shoulder. He gently turned me around. When we were face to face, his smile was mischievous.

"No, James, I mean it. I've got no time to play tiddlywinks."

"Baby, I'm not tryin' to get your motor runnin'. I'm here for something else." I put my hands on my hips and gave James my go-ahead, let's keep-talking nod. "You know what Professor Swede said...about Alicia going away to school." I nodded, again. "Sugar Plum, we've got to decide. Does she, or doesn't she?"

I looked down at my hands then back up at my husband. "We need to do what's best for our daughter."

James took my hand in his. "Professor Swede says Alicia's scholastically advanced for her age."

"I know, I know. She needs more challenges than the professor's school can give." I squeezed James' hand. "What do you think?"

He looked at me, and I could see the answer in his eyes. The next week, upon Professor Swede's recommendation, Alicia was sent to a female Negro finishing school in Austin, Texas. So many thoughts rushed through my mind I had trouble concentrating on the occasion at hand. What was worse? Losing your home, your parents or your daughter? Of course, Alicia wasn't going away forever, but I still had that same tight feeling in my throat, that a person gets when they hope everything will turn out all right but know something bad is going to happen. As Alicia boarded the train, I waved "goodbye" thinking "Good luck, girl.

Know thyself and stay strong."

****

The English poet, Alexander Pope, got it exactly right when he wrote, 'Swiftly fly the years'. I can add to Pope's poem that as we age, the days and weeks and months fly by even more swiftly. It was early April 1921. Alicia was away at school in Austin. James was with his army buddies for their weekly poker game at Willard's Billiard Parlor.

That evening, I was in attendance at Professor Swede's. The lecturer was a young physicist by the name of Enrico Fermi, who had just published his first scientific work in an Italian journal. Signore Fermi, who was on sabbatical from Normale school in Pisa, Italy, had a rudimentary command of the English language, but what he lacked in clear pronunciation he more than made up for in sign-language. After Professor Fermi's discourse, I stood in front of the man from Italy, and asked, "You say everything is relative? Everything?"

"Si, of course," he answered, waving his arms in the air for emphasis. "To paraphrase Trotsky, "Everything is relative, only change endures."

That night lying in bed, while James was still at Williards, relativity was still ricocheting through my mind. "If everything is relative, then everything is a lie. And if everything's a lie, then everything's permitted." I fell asleep in a nihilistic funk and dreamt about clocks, hundreds of them, big ones, little ones, all ticking like they were counting off time until the end of the world. But instead of the clock's hands going forward in time, they were spinning counterclockwise, all the way back to when I was a ten-year-old girl, blissfully sitting under the branches of my lilac tree. Then, like Devils loosed from hell, hooded men came riding skeletal horses. My heart started pounding hard and kept beating like it would explode. I screamed then woke up in a cold sweat. Someone opened the front door and closed it shut.

"James?"

There wasn't an immediate answer. I picked up the pistol laying on my nightstand. Slowly, the bedroom door opened. Even in the dark, I recognized his face and let loose a sigh of relief.

"James. Thank God, it's you."

"You were expecting the boogieman, maybe?"

James walked over to the nightstand next to the bed. He

pulled the cord hanging from the electric lamp. I was more than relived to see his big smile.

"Of course not," I huffed, then carefully placed the .32 back on it proper place.

"I heard you scream. Everything okay?"

I untangled myself from the sheets and sat up in bed. "Oh, James, it was terrible."

He sat on the edge of the bed, and asked, "Another one of those nightmares, huh?"

James stroked my arm. His voice was soft and comforting. "Now, now, Baby. Take it easy. It was just a dream, right? We all have them. Nothing bad really happened. Probably just indigestion. Maybe you should take a break from Mister Swede's lectures, huh?"

I twisted a hanky in my hands, and whispered, "I wish I knew what it meant. Why, after all these years, is that horrible day resurfacing? It seems almost like…like a premonition."

James shrugged and kept the phony smile plastered on his face. "C'mon, Olivia, don't be trying to find signs in tea leaves. I know it must've been hard on you…having your home burned to the ground. But lighting never strikes the same house twice. Isn't that what Mama used to say?"

CHAPTER TWENTY-FOUR
NIGHT VISIONS

When I walked into Mama's old kitchen, I found Professor Swede just where I expected, sitting in his wheelchair. The old man's head was bent over so far, his chin was resting on his chest. A kerosene lantern salvaged from the long-ago Missouri fire provided illumination. He held a magnifying glass in his hand and seemed to be engrossed in a book lying open on his lap. But then, like he was one of those mechanical automatons at a penny-arcade, Professor Swede slowly lifted his head and turned in my direction.

"Olivia," he wheezed.

"Hello, Professor Swede. Don't you think you should use more light when reading?"

"Bah, at my age I'm half blind. A ten-thousand watt light bulb wouldn't make a bit of difference. So, my dear girl, what brings you?"

"I've brought you a meal on wheels. Look." I pointed to the little red wagon I was pulling behind me. "I have all your favorites. Italian salami, hard-boiled duck eggs, pickled pig's feet, cheddar cheese, sardines, crackers and two bottles of that carbonated soda you like so well."

"Ah, Coca-Cola?" He licked his parched lips.

"Of course. One for you and one for me."

"Olivia, you spoil me."

Clamping an opener on a can of sardines, I asked, "How's the ankle, Professor?"

150

"Not too bad. It's all day sitting in a wheelchair that's killing me."

"Well if you hadn't—"

"Hadn't climbed on that ladder this would never had happened. I've heard that a million times, now, what's for lunch?"

Once I'd had the slimy sardines exposed, I laid one across a cracker and handed it to Professor Swede. As always, he graciously accepted my offering, then I made an open-face sardine sandwich for myself.

I took a sip of the carbonated soda. "Wow, that stuff goes right up your nose."

"I like to put salted peanuts in my Coca Cola," Professor Swede commented.

He finished off two more sardine sandwiches, then put the bottle of Coca-Cola to his lips. As he chugged the contents without taking a breath, the sight of his Adams apple bouncing up and down inside his skinny neck put a grin on my face. The professor finally placed the empty bottle on the table, let out a sizable belch, then focused on me.

"Out with it, Olivia. I appreciate the meal with wheels, but you didn't come here just for a sardine sandwich, now did you?"

I stared back at my old friend and shook my head. "I…I don't know what to think, Professor Swede. James says it's just a dream. But sometimes dreams come true, don't they?"

"What on earth are you talking about, Olivia?"

I gave Professor Swede all the details of my dream concerning hooded men, skeletal horses, and burning houses. He leaned over with a grunt and shuffled through a pile of books sitting on the chair next to him. When he finally found the right one, he placed it on the one that was already open on his lap.

Pointing to the book, Professor Swede declared, "Sigmund Freud's The Interpretation of Dreams. For you to understand the significance of your nightly hallucinations, you must read Freud's work. It's all explained between the covers."

Professor Swede handed the tome to me. "Oh, Professor, I wish there was more time in a twenty-four-hour day, but I'm already drowning in other projects."

He lowered his blue watery eyes. "I understand, Olivia. Life can be overwhelming but to ignore these nightmares will only lead to more complications."

I handed the book back to Professor Swede. "You've read Freud, Professor - maybe you can interpret the dream's meaning for me?"

Professor Swede shifted his weight in the wheelchair and wheeled it closer to me. "Doctor Freud asserts that a dream is an unfilled wish."

"Why would I wish for something so vile and horrible to happen, again? Once was bad enough, don't you think?"

Professor Swede tapped his long skinny forefinger on the cover of Freud's book. "The nightmare is a distorted rendition of reality that you wish will never happen, again. Somehow though, this dreadful vision, like a broken record, is stuck in a repetitious groove."

"But why?" I pleaded. "Why is this tormenting me, now? It all happened so long ago. My God, don't tell me, does my dream mean my house will be destroyed, again?"

Professor Swede shrugged. "Freud says that dreams, good or bad, are a reflection on the past, not a portent of the future. But there are some, me included, who think otherwise."

****

On the evening of May 29th 1921, I guided my husband into the parlor, took his hat and pointed to the camel-back sofa. On a side table sat a cold bucket of beer and two glass drinking mugs. When we were comfortably seated next to each other, I clinked my mug full of the golden-brown illegal beverage against his, and announced, "Happy birthday, James."

We laughed and quaffed the malty tasting suds, wiping white foam from our upper lips. James let out a satisfied groan. "Mmmmm, now that's what I call, good."

"The owner of Two-Ten Saloon brewed it. He calls it a veggie-beer. I traded him endives and sweet peas for the next batch. It's darker than usual, but it tastes great."

James placed his empty mug on the table and leaned over for a kiss. When he pulled back, he shook his head. "Mmmmm...mmmm, endive beer. Who would have ever thought that we'd be living like white folks? What's next on the menu, caviar with smoked finnan haddie?"

I refilled James' mug with veggie-beer. "Well, Slugger, tonight it's pot roast with carrots and potatoes. Tomorrow who knows, chicken feathers, maybe?"

He reached over to pull me onto his lap, and whispered, "Tomorrow will be a better day. No more nightmares, okay?"

I leaned back against James' broad chest and sighed, "Okay."

"Don't worry, Sweetheart," James said, kissing my lips. "Nothin's gonna' change your world, not if I've got any say about it."

****

Monday May 30th, 1921 started out just like every other morning; crispy bacon, burned toast, eggs sunny-side-up and Hills Brothers Coffee minus the chicory, black with two lumps of sugar. My hard-working husband gobbled down his food, gave me a quick peck on the cheek and left the house to open Rose's Grocery #1. I cleaned up the breakfast mess, grabbed my purse and went outside, where I hailed a jitney. Fifteen minutes later, I gave the driver five cents with a penny tip and went inside Rose's Grocery #2. Banana John was waiting for me with clipboard in hand.

"Good-a morning, Miss Olivia. Mamma Mia don' you look-a snazzy today."

I twirled around a couple of times, giving Banana John a three-hundred-sixty degree perspective of my new pin-stripe blouse with its high white collar, cuffs and metal buttons. Cinched at the waist with a wide black belt, I thought the matching dress made me look at least ten pounds lighter than usual.

I rolled my eyes and whispered, "James would blow his top if he knew what I paid for this outfit."

"What-ever you-a pay, is darn well worth it. Now, you ready to do-a the weekly order?"

I nodded and followed Banana John to the back of the store. At exactly 10:30 a.m. after the order for produce had been placed to Giuseppe in Saint Louis, the bell on the front door tinkled.

"Damn-a-it all to hell," Banana John grumbled and started to rise from his chair. "I thought I locked the door."

I quickly rose to my feet. "You stay, I'll get it."

Ten minutes later, when I returned to the office, Banana John looked up at me. He slowly moved the ever-present stogie from one corner of his mouth to the other side. "Whas-sa matter wit' you? Not sick, are you? You look like you just seen a ghost."

Slowly I sunk down onto a chair and shook my head.

"That was the milkman. Something terrible has happened in downtown Tulsa."

"What happened? Somebody got shot?"

"No, it seems a Negro shoeshine boy got into trouble."

Banana John shrugged. "Nothin' unusual about that, is there?"

"They're charging him with assaulting a white woman."

Banana John's bushy salt and pepper eyebrows were knitted together. His smile had faded to a frown. "Now that's gonna make-a a big problem for everybody."

****

I left Rose's #2 and during the jitney ride north toward the commissary kitchen, I thought about how events get blown way out of proportion, especially if the situation concerns a Negro boy and a white woman. Once I'd arrived at my destination, I started preparing one-hundred ready-to-eat meals of cornbread, black-eyed peas and grits. While placing the carry-out food in cardboard containers lined with wax paper, the shocking news coming out of Tulsa was forgotten and shoved in the box with the cornbread.

When I braked the wagon to a stop in front of Jerome's Never Closes it was almost 2:00 p.m. One of Jerome's hired hands unloaded the boxes of pre-packaged meals while I went inside the theater where I saw my brother talking to a man holding a wooden dummy that wore a tiny top hat and a tuxedo, two sizes too small.

Jerome said, "I'm sorry, Mister Lester, but ventriloquists are a dime a dozen. Besides, I've never seen such an ugly face on a dummy."

"But, Mister Truluck. My act is different." Mister Lester nodded at the dummy. "Thurston Powell the Third isn't ugly, he just has a lot of exposed personality. Look at the knothole on his forehead." Like he was proud of his handiwork, Mister Lester puffed out his chest. "I carved him myself."

"Uh-huh," Jerome grunted. "Okay, I'm a sucker for new acts. Let's see what you got. But make it snappy, I've got six more lined up behind you."

Using his free hand, Mister Lester pulled a pack of pre-rolled cigarettes from his jacket, then stuck one between his lips and lit it with a wooden kitchen match. Jerome and I watched in amazement as Thurston Powell the Third sang the words to the U. S. National Anthem, while Mister Lester puffed away without moving his lips, well, not very much. What made his act even more interesting was when the dummy recited the Gettysburg Address, while the ventriloquist gargled water.

When Mister Lester finished his audition, he was hired on the spot. Ever the thoughtful brother, Jerome escorted me out of the theater. It was while we were standing next to the wagon that I reported the morning events concerning the young Negro man who had supposedly accosted a white woman.

My brother took my hands in his and whispered, "It only takes one spark to start a conflagration."

CHAPTER TWENTY-FIVE
RUMORS OF WAR

That evening I delivered Professor Swede his meal-on-wheels dinner, then hurried home to prepare a man-sized meal for my man. In no time James consumed a two-inch thick T-bone steak, a mound of garlic smashed potatoes, boiled beet greens and strawberry-vanilla tapioca for dessert. When the smile on his face told me that his stomach was full, I scooted my chair closer. I slipped my arm around my husband's neck and put my lips close to his ear.

"I want to try something different," I whispered.

"What do you have in mind?"

"This," I said, and produced a hand-rolled cigarette.

"Where did that come from?"

"Jerome gave it to me. I told him about my nightmare. He says it will settle my sand."

James pulled back and looked at me. "Sweetheart, what do you have to be worried about? Business is booming. What's more, we just got a report on how well Alicia's doing in school. I don't understand. Why do you need the Mary Jane?" He took the cigarette from my fingers. "C'mon, Baby, tell me, what's really bothering you."

I shook my head, again. "I don't know, it's just something I feel. That young Negro boy who they claim attacked a white woman this morning, that really worries me. Maybe we should leave Greenwood. Go on a little vacation. Just for a few days. We'll take the train to Austin and visit Alicia."

"Who'll run the grocery stores? Who'll feed Jerome's Never Closes famished mob? No, Baby," James said, shaking his head. "I'm afraid we're tied down right here. At least for now."

I silently studied the floral pattern on the wallpaper behind James. Finally, when my woman's intuition got the best of me, I whispered, "Even if we did go somewhere, I wonder if there'd be anything left to come back to."

****

Tuesday morning, May 31, 1921, before James left the house to open Rose's Grocery #1, the telephone hanging on the wall in the hallway started buzzing. The buzz stopped when James picked up the receiver. After a few muffled words, he came into the kitchen, where I was cleaning up the breakfast dishes.

"That was Jerome," James said, his voice sounding serious. "The boy involved in the altercation is Dick Roland. He's a shoeblack who goes by the moniker, Diamond Dick."

"A Negro with an offensive nickname who bumped into a white woman by accident. Did Jerome have any more news.?"

"Roland's nineteen-years-old. He was downtown at his shoeshine stand when he went into the Drexel Building to use the colored restroom."

"Isn't that all the way up on the fifth or sixth floor?"

James nodded. "When Mister Roland stepped into the elevator, they say he tripped and accidently bumped into the operator."

"Whose name is...?"

"...Sara Paige. She's claiming that Roland jumped her like a tomcat in heat."

"Oh, baloney. Whoever heard of anything so ridiculous, and on an elevator? Why, if Mister Roland wanted to get into trouble, I can think of a million other devious plots that would be more subtle. A Negro male molesting a white female in broad daylight, in a public place...that's absurd."

"You're right about that," James said, snagging a piece of bacon for the road. "It seems the Tulsa sheriff has issued an arrest warrant for Mister Roland."

I set the white porcelain cup I was holding down on the table so hard the black coffee sloshed over the side. "To arrest a man solely on the word of a hysterical woman, no matter what their color, without first getting the details that a crime has been committed, why, that's…that's unconstitutional."

"Tell that to Sheriff Willard McCullough," James said, and rushed out the door.

****

At 3:30 p.m., I was sitting in the darkened parlor of my home with a wet dish towel on my forehead, trying to relieve a pounding headache that wouldn't go away. I'd already made the box lunches for Jerome's Never Closes and needed to start preparing dinner. After that, I would go to bed and collapse. All day, I'd been asking myself over and over, "Since when is accidently stepping on a white woman's toe considered an assault? What if the shoe had been on the other foot? What if the elevator operator had been a Negro woman and a white man bumped into her? He'd either offer a quick apology, or accuse the woman of rape, and that would be the end of the story." I came to the conclusion that unless everyone in the country of my birth accepted the fact that all men are created equal, then nothing will change, ever. When the afternoon newspaper landed on the front porch with a loud thud, I snapped out of my reverie.

There was no time to read the latest gossip, so I left the bird cage liner where it landed and went into the kitchen. I heard the front door open and James' familiar footsteps as he walked into the parlor. I had just finished peeling six russet potatoes to add to a broccoli casserole when my dearly beloved husband came in the kitchen and took his chosen seat at the table.

He pointed to the newspaper he was holding and asked, "Have you read today's paper?"

"No, I haven't had the time."

James read the Tribune's headline out loud. "'Authorities nab Negro for Attacking Girl in Elevator'."

"How can they print something like that if nothing's been proven? Have you ever heard of anything so ridiculous?"

James shook his head and folded the newspaper into a very small square. "Whether it's the truth, or not, the press will print whatever sells newspapers."

"But when the white people read this, they'll want to…"

"Lynch the kid," James hissed.

****

After James and I finished dinner that evening we went to bed with the chickens. When we heard someone banging on our front door, James switched on the electric table lamp, and grumbled, "Who can that be at this ungodly hour?"

I rubbed my eyes and guessed, "Probably Professor Swede. Sometimes he rolls across the street in that wheelchair." When I looked at the Regulator wall clock it read 9:45 p. m.

"How does he manage to get that thing up on the porch?" James asked, slipping on the silk embroidered housecoat that I'd given him for his birthday.

I shrugged. "Maybe he takes wing."

"Uh-huh," James grunted his nonreply as he walked out the door.

I checked the wall clock, again. Ten minutes had elapsed since James left our bedroom, and he still hadn't returned. I rolled out of bed, dropped a wool poncho over my head and headed for the parlor. Jerome was standing by the fireplace with a glass of wine in his hand. James was seated on the sofa, elbows on his knees, looking down at a spot on the floor. When he raised up, my husband looked at me then he took a drink from his half-filled tumbler. I assumed the brownish-colored liquid was bourbon.

I took a seat next to James, pointed at the glass in his hand, and asked, "Isn't it a little late for that?"

"Jerome says there's trouble brewing," James said. "After the Roland boy was arrested, he was taken to the Tulsa County Courthouse. The sheriff put the kid up on the second floor. Now, there's a crowd of whites outside the jail maybe a couple of hundred or so, all clamoring for Roland's neck."

"Isn't there such a thing as a trial by your peers?" I asked.

Ignoring my rhetorical question, Jerome blurted, "There's gonna' be big-time trouble, Olivia. I saw the whole thing for myself. Those white vigilantes are frothing at the mouth for blood. Acting just like rabid skunks, they are. Whitey is stinkin' up the place, hollering for Diamond Dick's neck."

"Jerome," I said, my voice low and demanding. "What were you doing in Tulsa?"

"A couple of my army buddies came to the theater this evening. They were looking for a few brave men. So, I went with them." Jerome polished off his wine in one gulp and shook his head. "It's a mob down there alright just itchin' to lynch that Roland kid."

"We've got to do something before all this gets out of hand," James said. "Let's round up some men and go down there to set the record straight."

"What?" I shrieked. "Are you crazy?"

James turned to me and lifted my chin. He looked me straight in the eyes. "You knew I didn't have all my marbles when you married me. For goodness sake, Olivia, I was a baseball player, somebody who's head is a non-moving target for a ninety-mile-per-hour fastball. But tonight, if we don't go to the courthouse and stop this tragedy from happening, those white devils are going to hang that boy and that would be murder. We can't let them do that, can we?" I stared at James and shook my head "no". "Good. Jerome and I can take care of ourselves. Once those white men see we're not fooling around, that we're dead serious about all this, they'll back down, right Jerome?"

Jerome shook his head and whispered, "I sure hope so."

"Okay, then," I huffed. "There's no way on God's green earth that I'm going to stay home, while my husband and brother put themselves in harm's way. If you two are going, then I am, too."

"No, Olivia," James ordered. "And that's final. If I have to tie you up, I…"

"Give me one good reason why I can't go."

"Let her go," Jerome said. "She can drive the Packard and stay with my poor baby."

Without waiting for James to respond, I rushed into the bedroom, threw on a pair of old corduroy trousers and one of James' flannel shirts. Five minutes later, I was sitting behind the steering wheel of the Packard. With James in the passenger seat and my brother in the rumble seat, I drove all the way down Greenwood Avenue without stopping and double-parked in front of Jerome's 24-hour theater. Cars and wagons filled with Negro men lined the curb. It was a strange sight to see a crowd of males and nobody cracking a joke.

One of the men climbed on the hood of a Model T, cupped his hands to his mouth, and shouted, "Sheriff McCullough has stationed armed guards in the courthouse."

Someone who was standing on the seat of a buckboard, hollered out, "There's seven deputies and over three hundred whites."

"Save Dick Roland," The man in the Model T roared, raising his fist in the air.

Another man wearing the white collar of the clergy raised his voice in warning, "Violence begets violence. They want us to come looking for trouble. We must show solidarity and determination, yes, yet keep our tempers under control. The whites would like nothing better than an excuse to shoot a Mister Roland, or a Negro, any Negro."

A tall man dressed in a World War I Army uniform, with an array of multi-colored medals dangling on his chest, chanted, "C'mon, c'mon, c'mon. What are we waiting for, men? Damn the torpedoes, full speed ahead. Save Dick Roland."

A booming roar of approval erupted from the ever-increasing crowd. There was an even louder rumble when they all started their car engines at the same time. I pulled away from the curb and wheeled the Packard south on Greenwood Avenue. When the car rumbled across the Frisco railroad tracks, I felt my heart migrate from my chest up into my throat. A couple of blocks further south, the parade of automobiles and wagons made a right turn on East First Street. We all headed Southwest until we came to Denver Street, where we turned south, again. We hadn't gone more than a couple of city blocks when the procession came to a halt. Jerome hopped out of the rumble seat, ran toward the front of the long line, only to return a few minutes later.

"They've got the road blocked up ahead. From here we go on foot."

James opened the passenger door. Before stepping out of the car he turned to look at me. My husband wore a grim expression on his face when he commanded, "Olivia you stay put. Hear me?"

"But, James, I…"

"No buts, ifs or ands about it. Who knows what we're going to run into. I can't take care of myself and you at the same time."

"He's right," Jerome agreed, running his hand across the shiny metal of the roadster's front fender. "You stay here and guard my baby."

"Please?" James begged. "You're a smart woman, someone who always listens to reason. When it comes to people of color, whites fly off the handle for no reason. But there may be a few who understand the economics of the situation."

"Which is?" I asked.

"A lynch mob hanging a young Negro boy can't be good for anybody's business, White or Negro, get it?"

"All right," I huffed and sat back in the seat. "But if you two aren't back soon, I'm coming after you."

Jerome chuckled and tipped his derby. "I'll be damned if she doesn't mean it, James. Let's hope she stays put for Whitey's sake."

James shook his head and muttered, "She is a ball of fire, alright."

CHAPTER TWENTY-SIX
BLACK WALL STREET BURNING

I never was one to chew on my fingernails, at least not until that night when I gnawed on a thumbnail while watching James and Jerome walk down the street, turn the corner and disappear out of sight. Finally, discontinuing what Mama used to call "A disgusting habit," I gripped the Packard's steering wheel with both hands and bowed my head.

"Dear Lord," I whispered, "I know I haven't talked to You as often as I should. Mama always told me to pity those who only speak to You when they want something. So please, Lord, I'm begging You, take pity on me. Please watch over James and Jerome. They're both good men who never harmed a living soul. Keep them safe from injury and protect that poor boy who's in jail. Thank you in advance, oh Lord. Amen."

The Packard was parked under three illuminated spheres suspended over the entrance to a pawn shop. Besides a bicycle and three guitars, a double-barrel shotgun was proudly displayed in the window. I sat staring at the deadly weapon while listening to the deathly silence coming from the direction of the courthouse. Finally, after what seemed like an eternity, human figures emerged from the mist. With bowed heads, the silent Negro men slowly shuffled past the Packard. The small watch pinned to the pocket of my shirt read 10:00 p.m. More and more men returned to climb back into their automobiles and wagons. I scooted forward in my seat, straining my eyes, hoping to spot James and Jerome. When the two appeared, I let out a big sigh of relief. This time James climbed into the rumble seat and Jerome took a place next to me. Not wanting to spend one more second than necessary parked inside the Tulsa City Limits, I gunned the Packard to life and made a tight U-turn.

I turned toward Jerome to ask, "Is the Roland boy okay?"

Jerome nodded. "The sheriff cleared all the whites from inside the courthouse. Roland is on the second floor. The armed guards are in there to make sure no one sneaks upstairs. Plus, they cut off the power to the elevator. We saw the kid from the outside. He was peeking through the bars on the window, smiling even. It didn't look like he'd been harmed."

"Give it time and things will cool down," James chimed in. "The sheriff promised that nothing would happen to Roland."

"And you believe him?" I asked.

I looked in the rearview mirror to see James lean forward. "Tell me, Olivia. At this point, what other choice do we have?"

When the Packard crossed the Frisco tracks, I let out another huge sigh of relief, and complained, "Well, I don't like any of it. Not one little bit. Trusting a white man to guard a Negro boy is like asking a moonshiner to stop making bootleg liquor."

"In other words," James said. "It ain't gonna' happen, right Sis?"

"That's right. And I'm telling you on more thing, no good will come from any of this."

"Amen," both men mumbled.

****

I parked the Packard in front of our house and slid out of the driver's seat. The emotional trauma coupled with the lack of sleep had left me exhausted in body and mind. The same thought kept drumming itself inside my head, "What if it had been James or Jerome who accidently bumped into a white woman? That could be my husband sitting in a Tulsa jail, depending on a white sheriff to keep a mob from dragging him to the nearest tree." My brain was in a fog, weighted down with worry, but I managed to overcome inertia and shuffled inside the house, made a pot of coffee for James, Jerome and the dozen or so other veterans who had followed us home. Like they hadn't eaten a decent meal in days, the hungry troops devoured leftover box lunches. When I finished cleaning up, it was well after midnight. There was standing room only in my parlor. The men were discussing their next move, but I was too worn-down to stay and listen. I headed to my bedroom hoping to catch forty-winks when the telephone in the hallway buzzed two longs and a short.

"Hello?"

"Miss Olivia?"

"Banana John?"

"That's right. I call to tell-a you something very important. Things are going from real bad to even worse in Tulsa."

"What do you mean?"

"White people. There's more and more comin' from-a all over the state."

"My God," I gasped. "They'll hang that boy."

After thanking Banana John, I hurried to the parlor, and announced, "The courthouse is surrounded by hundreds of whites."

One of the vets spoke up. "I knew it. They're gonna' hang Diamond Dick. My cousin deserves a fair trial."

Shouting profanities, Jerome and the rest of the men stormed out of the house. James headed toward our bedroom. When I stood in the doorway, I saw my husband holding a double-barrel shotgun under the nub of his right arm, loading shells into the twin chambers with his left hand.

"Please, James," I begged. "Stay here. Don't go."

"I have to," he said, closing the shotgun's barrel with a metallic snap. "We've got to take a stand, or they'll keep railroading us, over and over. Tulsa looks as good a place to start as any."

"I'm…"

"No, you are not. Not this time. You will stay here and wait until I get back. And don't argue, hear?"

"But…"

"Olivia, if I have to, I'll tie you to the bed post." He lifted my chin so I could look into his kind eyes. "Please, just keep the home-fires burning. That's all I ask. We've been down this road before. Don't worry, Baby, I'll be back."

****

I finally relented and slowly shuffled back to the kitchen. Too tired to pour myself a cup of cold coffee, I sat at the table and looked at the Regulator Wall Clock hanging on the wall. It read 3:00 a.m. As the old timepiece kept ticking over and over like a hypnotic metronome, I rested my forehead on the table and was soon fast asleep.

I dreamt I was back in Missouri, walking along the Tebo Creek. It was a beautiful day. There wasn't a cloud in the sky. A warm breeze caressed my face. I stopped to pick up a perfectly round flat stone, then just like Daddy had showed me, I threw the rock so that it skipped across the smooth water a half-dozen times. I kept walking downstream, until I saw Mama far in the distance. Her mouth was moving like she was trying to tell me something, but she was too far away for me to hear. I rushed toward Mama, but she evaporated into the mist. My eyes popped open when the grandfather clock in the hallway chimed six times.

I lifted my head and jumped to my feet, calling out, "James? James, is that you?"

There was no answer. I hurried though the house and stepped out on the front porch. In the light of a false dawn, I looked South. Plumes of black smoke were swirling high in the air. Then from high over my head there came a loud buzzing sound. I looked up to see two biplanes flying low over the rooftops. A woman running north on Greenwood Avenue screamed, "Run for your life afore it's too late. They're killin' all the colored people."

I was shocked to see that the street was filled with Negros of all ages heading North. I hurried down to the sidewalk. An old man having a coughing and wheezing fit, was leaning against the lamppost. It looked as though he was about ready to tumble out onto the street, so I let him lean on my shoulder.

"Mister, are you alright."

"Good Lord Almighty," the man sobbed. He gasped for his next breath of air. "I ain't never seen nothin' like it, not in all my born days."

"What in the world is happening?"

"The end of the world," he puffed, then had to take in a couple of deep breaths before continuing. "The white folks have gone plain nuts. They's shootin' Negros right and left...no questions asked. They's burnin' down all the buildings, too. Them airplanes are droppin' turpentine on the fires. You better run, Missy. Don't go down there. They's dead bodies layin' everywhere."

"What about the men who are saving Dick Roland?"

"Don't know nothin' 'bout them folks," the old man

166

rasped. "My guess is they's all done for, too."

A young man rushed up and gently took the old man's arm, "C'mon, Gran'daddy, we got to keep movin'. No way we can stay here." When the kid looked at me there was unmitigated fear in his big brown bug eyes. "Ain't never seen nothin' like this. It's downright murder."

I turned and hurried back to the house, thinking, "Negro Wall Street's burning? White men shooting Negros? No, no, no…that's not right. None of that is right. It can't be happening. Not here. Not in America. Not in the Greenwood District. We're civilized people, aren't we?" By the time I got back to the house, I was talking out loud, "I've got to find James and Jerome. It'll take too long if I hitch up the surrey or start the Model T. I'll just ride Cicero."

Ten minutes later I had saddled James's chestnut gelding and was picking my way down Greenwood Avenue while trying to avoid the tide of humanity coming my way. I hadn't gone but a couple of blocks when I heard a buzzing sound. Up in the sky, a biplane skimmed over the rooftops. When the pilot banked to the right, Cicero and I must have made an inviting target because he aimed the flying merchant of death directly at us.

I froze, my mouth hanging wide open as the biplane flew closer and closer, until finally it came close enough that if I stood on the saddle, I might've been able to touch the plane's round wheels. The pilot wore a leather helmet and goggles with a white scarf wrapped around his neck that flapped in the breeze. Occupying the seat behind him, another helmeted man tossed something round over the side of the plane's fuselage. The burning sphere spiraled down to earth like an errant 4th of July Roman candle. Upon impact the incendiary device exploded. The flash was close enough that I could feel the heat emanating from an orange-tinged ball of fire.

Searching for more profitable targets, the plane continued flying South toward the heart of Negro Wall Street. Finally, I was able to close my mouth and unclench my colon. I spurred Cicero forward until I was two city blocks away from Archer Street and Greenwood Avenue where my horse reared, almost ditching me in the gutter. Tightening the reins and clamping down on Cicero's bit, I turned to see a figure stumbling toward me, hollering, "Help me. Help, I'm burning up."

Before I could dismount to help the poor man, he collapsed in the street, his entire body engulfed in flames. The sweet stench of burning flesh assaulted my nose. In the distance, I could see a crowd of white men headed in my direction. Shots rang out and bullets started whizzing over my head. Then a flatbed truck with a machine gun mounded in back, barreled in from a side street, stopping in front of the white mob. Immediately more gunfire erupted. The whites were targeting the soldiers on the flatbed. The driver gunned the motor and headed north on Greenwood Avenue. Shots were fired from the Negros manning hastily built barricades. The flatbed quickly turned off on a side street and disappeared from view.

Someone yelled, "Save Mount Zion." A group of Negro men rushed by, heading for the steps of the Mount Zion Baptist Church. When the screaming sound of sirens could be heard the white offensive seemed to stall.

"The Tulsa Fire Department," someone hollered. "Help is on the way."

Any hopes for an end to the hostilities were dashed when more whites joined the fray. Warning shots were fired at the fire trucks. The firemen beat a hasty retreat. So did I. My path to Tulsa had been blocked by an invading white army intent on slaughtering the young, old, male or female, just as long as they were Negro. As I threaded my way back North on Greenwood Avenue, from behind a great shadow fell over me. The buzzing sound told me it was another biplane looking for targets.

Cicero and I took shelter from the flying machines under the branches of an elm tree, which gave me a brief moment to organize my thoughts. "The Germans occupied France and Belgium. Now, white barbarians who are invading Greenwood. It doesn't mae sense. How can a man indiscriminately kill another man? They're behaving like wild animals...no, this is worse. Animals kill to eat these men are killing for their own pleasure."

Once the sky was clear of biplanes, I spurred Cicero home, where I rushed into the bedroom. Inside the closet, I picked up the rifle that was leaning against the wall. A solitary shaft of sunlight streamed through the window causing the polished brass receiver gleam. I made sure the .44 caliber Henry was fully loaded with sixteen rimfire brass cartridges then hefted the seven-pound weapon on my shoulder. Marching through the kitchen, I grabbed a wedge of burned cornbread from off stove and hurried out the front door.

I rushed across the street. When I stepped inside Mama's house, I went from room to room until I found Professor Swede in the kitchen. The poor man was trying to light the gas stove, but his palsied hand was shaking so much he couldn't strike a kitchen match.

I leaned the rifle against the counter and gently took the matches. "I'm sorry, Professor, but we don't have time for coffee."

"Going hunting, are we?" he asked, turning his attention to the Henry.

I shook my head vigorously. "White people are rioting. They've set Negro Wall Street on fire and they're coming this way...shooting Negros and burning buildings." I nodded toward the antique Henry. "I want to be prepared."

"Ah yes, the motto of the Boy Scouts. Nothing wrong with taking planned action."

That's when the telephone hanging on the wall started buzzing two shorts and one long. "Oh, God, I hope that's James." I rushed over to pick up the receiver.

The voice on the other end of the telephone line belonged to Banana John. After a brief exchange of words, I placed the receiver back on its hook. The clock on the wall read 9:00 a.m. My whole body felt numb as if I'd been drafted in a daytime nightmare with no hope of escape. My eyes rested on Professor's Swede's trembling hands.

"Banana John said the Tulsa Police have deputized dozens of white men. Any Negro resisting arrest will be shot on sight. Those men who went to the courthouse have been rounded-up and sent to a detention camp. That means that James and Jerome...good God, maybe they're still alive."

Professor Swede exclaimed, "Men taken into custody for peacefully protesting? Negros being shot and killed for no apparent reason? For, God's sake, Olivia. Where is the law?"

I tried to hold back the tears, but they oozed out anyway. "Banana John said that Mama's store has been burned to the ground. That means Number One will be next." I looked at Professor Swede, then at the Henry rifle leaning against the chair. "We've got to get out of here, Professor. If we stay, they'll kill us."

The old professor shook his head and muttered something

about, "The Barbarians have crossed the Frisco tracks."

CHAPTER TWENTY-SEVEN
TULSA MASSACRE

Without uttering a peep, Professor Swede sat stiffer than a wooden Indian and held the Henry rifle at port arms. I gripped the handles on the wheelchair so hard that my knuckles turned white, then pushed the cumbersome wheelie out the backdoor onto the porch. Close to the edge of the steps, I leaned the chair back to balance it on two wheels, swiveled the whole contraption around one-hundred-eighty degrees, held on tight, then went backward down the three steps and let gravity do its work.

It was a rough bouncing down the steps. On the way, Professor Swede craned his head around, and asked, "Where to, Olivia?"

"A safe place," I grunted.

I drug the wheelchair backwards across the lawn, glad it hadn't rained in over a week. When I stopped to catch my breath, I looked toward the South. Giant black plumes of smoke billowed over the Greenwood District. Biplanes still buzzed overhead with the agility of natural birds, dropping turpentine bombs. With the wind blowing from the south, the air was filled with the acrid smell of burning oil and rubber. I tried not to inhale the noxious fumes deep into my lungs and kept pulling on the wheelchair.

Finally, we made it to the outhouse. I turned toward Mister Swede. In a calm voice, I said, "I'll take the rifle, Professor."

I leaned the Henry against the outhouse, worked my hands under the professor's arms and lifted. Once the frail old man was upright, I helped him shuffle over to the lilac tree.

"Now, Professor, you have to get down on all fours."

"What? Are you pulling my leg, Olivia?"

"Professor, you have to crawl inside the tree."

"But the hole is no bigger than a matchbox."

"Please, Professor," I begged, pulling the branches apart. "No more arguing. We have to hide, now."

While Professor Swede slowly wormed his body through the thick shrubbery, I stashed the wheelchair behind the outhouse. Once the two of us and the Henry rifle were well hidden beneath the lilac branches, I separated the foliage to keep an eye on Mama's place. There was no sign of the white rioters. I breathed a sigh of relief and scooted further in backward, to check on Professor Swede.

"Are you doing okay?" I whispered.

He licked his chapped lips and nodded. "I could use a drink of water."

"I'm sorry, Professor, but I forgot to--"

"Shhh," The Professor hissed. "Do you hear men's voices?"

I crawled back to my spyhole and peeked out to see two white men standing on Mama's back porch. The fools were talking and laughing like they owned the property. Then, without a warning, one of them aimed his rifle in our direction. I was certain we had been discovered. There was a loud bang, a white puff of smoke, then the sound of splintering wood.

"Damn him all to hell," I grumbled. "That cracker is using the outhouse for target practice. I've had just about all I can tolerate." In the heat of the moment, with my hormones stuck in overdrive, I stuck the barrel of the rifle through the branches, took aim, then sucked in a lungful of air like Daddy taught me. I let my breath out real slow. My finger gently rested on the trigger, and my lungs begged for relief. The thought went through my mind, "I've got the s.o.b. dead to rights. What's one less white man in the grand scheme of things?" Then, thankfully, common sense kicked in. "But, if I shoot, I'll expose our position and that will be the end of us." In the end, I decided that shooting a white man was not worth either me or Mister Swede getting killed. Finally, the man turned and went back inside the house. Minutes later black smoke started billowing from the open windows. I couldn't believe my eyes. Mama's place was going-up in flames. There was nothing I could do, so I laid on my belly and wet the dirt with my tears.

****

The watch pinned to my shirt read 4:00 p.m. There had been no sign of the marauders for a couple hours and except for the occasional popping of burning embers, there was total silence. Even the birds had quit singing. I slowly wormed my way out of our hiding place, then turned to tug on the professor who had dozed off. Once he had wriggled through the narrow opening, I retrieved the wheelchair from behind the outhouse, helped my dear old friend up onto the seat, and pulled him back across the lawn. There I stood dumfounded, staring at the smoldering ruins of Mama's house. With tears dripping down my cheeks, I took deep breath and screamed loud and long, almost to the point of losing consciousness. Finally, once I'd regained control of my emotions, I gritted my teeth and using all my strength, pushed Mister Swede to the front sidewalk. There, my worst fears were realized. All that was left of the home that James and I had built were a few charred pieces of lumber sticking out of the ground and the solitary brick chimney. In our front yard, laying on his side, was the carcass of Cicero. By this time, I had become faint. My legs felt like rubber. I couldn't take another step forward. And even if I could, where would I go? I fell down on the curb, buried my face in my hands and sobbed my heart out.

Professor Swede patted my back and tried to alleviate my sorrow. "Olivia, you and James are young and strong. You can rebuild. Your whole future awaits. Put all this tragedy behind you. Turn it into a new beginning."

I looked up at the Professor, and asked, "Do you mean like we did the last time?" There was no answer forthcoming. I wiped my runny nose with the back of my hand and muttered, "Gone. All gone, again."

"There, there, Olivia," he said, still patting my shoulder. "There, there."

"All the photographs. My hope chest. James's baseball glove. Daddy's corn cob pipes. Everything, it's all gone. Burned to the ground. And why? Just because our skin is black?"

The professor let out an audible sigh. "Olivia," he wheezed. "Hate is something that nobody in their right mind understands. If I've learned one thing about the inhuman race, it's that some people are just downright mean. They've got an ornery streak a mile wide. There's a deplorable class of people in this country who are uneducated and ill-informed. These are the sort of people who can't control their baser instincts. All it takes to start a conflagration is a spark."

"Yeah," I sighed, "I heard that before."

I finally found the strength to rise to my feet and looked down Greenwood Avenue. As far as the eye could see, the destruction was total. Where there once were brick buildings, now there was nothing but blackened walls and ashes. The people who had fled North were now starting to trickle back from their hiding places. What they hoped to find, I wasn't sure, because to me it didn't look like anything salvageable was left. There came the creak of wagon wheels. I turned to see Banana John. He was navigating around an overturned burned hulk of an automobile.

"Thank, God," I whispered. "A Sicilian angel to the rescue."

When he reined-in the two horses, Banana John shook his head back from side to side. "Thank God and all the saints. You're still among the living."

"James and Jerome," I blurted. "Do you have any word?"

"They're at the city park on Eleventh and Elgin Street with the rest of the Negro protestors."

"Thank God, again," I whimpered, a speck of joy returning to my battered heart.

"C'mon, Olivia," Banana John said. "We got to get you and the Mister Swede outta' here. I'll take you to my place. We'll find James and Mister Jerome, that's-a promise."

Wallowing his ever-present cigar, Banana John was able to lift Professor Swede up onto the flatbed wagon where he made the old man a comfortable place to rest. In the meantime, I ran back to the outhouse, knelt down on my knees and shoveled dirt with my hands like a dog digging for a bone. Once, I'd unearthed the metal coffee can, exactly where I'd buried it, I hurried to the wagon. Professor was lying on Mama's singed Oriental rug, fast asleep. I hoisted myself up on the front seat. Banana John clucked his tongue to get the two horses moving and aimed the wagon south on Greenwood Avenue.

Banana John said. "I found something for you."

He handed me a faded tintype blackened around the edges from the fire. I studied the white-haired Negro man in the sepia-colored photo and shook my head.

"You found Grandpa Truluck."

"It's-a good, now you-a got someone to remember of your family."

Banana John wallowed his cigar around, as he guided the wagon through the maze of overturned automobiles, trucks and wooden beer barrels.

"Daddy and Mama Rose will always be in my heart," I whispered.

CHAPTER TWENTY-EIGHT
EXODUS AGAIN

Greenwood Avenue was a blackened no-man's land. The once broad street was littered with burning tires, overturned jitneys and dead horses. When our wagon rolled past Jerome's Never Closes there was nothing left of the building, but an empty shell surrounded by charred, crumbling brick walls.

I had cried so much my tear ducts had gone dry. Now, my eyes burned, the inside of my mouth felt like mummy parchment, and when I spoke, my voice was a low monotone. "Everything is burned down to the ground. The hitching posts are nothing but charred matchsticks. Have the white people gone totally insane?"

"Look," Banana John said, pointing to the left. "They send-a in the army."

The intense sunlight reflected off polished gun barrels and bayonets. I shielded my eyes with my hand and flinched when I spied a flatbed truck with a machine gun pointing directly at me. I tried to swallow but with no spittle my tongue stuck to the roof of my mouth. The over-heated air was filled with the stench of burning oil and flesh. I covered my nose and mouth with one of Mama's old handkerchiefs and watched as the Oklahoma National Guard herded a group of Negro men in the same direction we were traveling. While we waited for the chain gang to pass by, I wanted to stand up and holler, "Those men did nothing wrong". But in the interest of self-preservation, I kept my mouth shut.

Banana John bent over to whisper, "You Negros will be blamed for this. They'll say it was-a your fault because you got-a too uppity."

"And too rich."

Thinking how history would interpret what happened on Negro Wall Street made me stomp my foot on the floorboard. "Nothing will be written about this. It will all be swept under the rug." I stewed in my juices for a minute or so, then huffed, "I want nothing more to do with Oklahoma. I'm through here."

"You mean you're gonna leave?"

"I'm going to buy a one-way ticket to anywhere but here." Then, I announced, "James and I will move to Texas where Alicia attends school. It's a big state. Maybe people there have bigger hearts."

We rode along in silence for a couple of blocks and when I glanced to my right the once beautiful marquee for the Williams Dreamland Theater had fallen and was laying on the ground in a heap. The theater's elaborately carved wooden doors were scorched but were still hanging on their hinges. The eerie landscape of lone brick chimneys that would never draw another fire, and charred telephone poles that would never carry another voice, made bleak sentinels to the horror that had transpired.

Suddenly, from behind, there was a loud Honk. I turned to see a horse-drawn wagon on our tail. Banana John reined in the horses and stopped next to a Model-T that had been flipped upside down. I gasped as the conveyance slowly rolled by, so close, I could see the flies buzzing around the bloodied, bruised faces of Negro corpses stacked three high.

As we started moving again, I whispered, "I wonder how many have been killed?"

Banana John wallowed the cigar stub from one corner of his mouth to the other. "Who knows? Maybe a-hundred maybe a thousand?"

"One would've been too many."

When we crossed the Frisco railroad track, Banana John kept going South until out of sheer habit, the horse stopped in front of his house. When I recognized the automobile that was parked on the street, my mouth dropped open.

"Jerome's Packard," I gushed. "It's still in one piece. But how did it get here?"

"Your brother left it for me to keep-a eye on," Banana John said, sliding off the wagon seat. "It's-a good thing, too. Nobody touch-a the machine or they answer to Banana John."

"Oh, oh, my back." Professor Swede was trying to sit up so he could scoot toward the front of the wagon. "That was a most unpleasant journey to say the least."

Once the professor was made comfortable inside Banana John's house, the produce man and I climbed back in the wagon and headed for the detention center at the Tulsa City Park.

Banana John turned to me, and with the ever-present stub of a Dutch Master cigar anchored in the corner of his mouth, he asked, "So, when we find James and Jerome – how we gonna get 'em out?"

"You're going to tell the authorities to release them into your custody. Remember when I first started working for you? Didn't you tell me that when you lived in Sicily, you were the chief of police."

"Well maybe I was, some of the time."

"But you showed me your badge."

"That was-a long time ago."

"Do you have the badge?"

Banana John nodded. "I always carry it, like-a lucky rabbit's foot."

"Okay then, Capo della Polizia Pusateri, it's time to arrest James and Jerome."

When Banana John and I were standing in front of the army captain in charge of the Negro detainees, the phony police chief impersonator flashed his badge and spoke in Italian.

"Il tempo oggi è bellissimo

The peach-fuzz captain-of-the-guard looked at me with question marks in his eyes, and commented, "I don't understand a word this man is saying."

"That's why I'm here, as Capo Pusateri's interpreter. He's been tracking two of your detainees for months. They're wanted on charges of extortion and smuggling fine art out of Italy. One is tall – about six-foot-two, has black curly hair that hangs down over his ears and goes by the name of James 'Handy' Bingham. The other thug is shorter and uglier. We've been informed he has a black eye and calls himself Jerome 'Licorice Stick' Truluck. Capo Pusateri traveled here all the way from Rome, Italy. He's been ordered to take these two criminals back for prosecution."

"I don't know if I can do that, Miss," the captain said, scratching his chin and eyeballing Banana John. "The men here are under arrest for disturbing the peace."

I turned to Banana John and said, "Questo potrebbe richiedere un po 'più di persuasione."

He smiled and replied, "Dagli entrambi i barili."

The captain was a few inches shorter than me, so I had to look down my nose at him. "How can you compare unruly public behavior with the crime of extorting widows out of their life savings and trying to heist great works of art? Do you want to be responsible for an international incident? If Capo Pusateri has to bring diplomatic action to arrest those two men, I assure you he will."

Once my husband and brother had been located, Capo Pusateri signed the official documents for their release, guaranteeing that the two prisoners would be promptly escorted back to Rome, Italy.

****

It had been two weeks since the 'Tulsa Massacre'. Not only had Negro Wall Street been obliterated but more than fifty square blocks of the Greenwood District had been turned to ashes. At the latest count, over three-hundred Negros had been murdered and hundreds more injured. James and I journeyed back to the rubble we once called home where we scavenged a few items and some charred clothing that would reek of smoke forever. Before leaving, I found a shovel and walked back to the outhouse to dig up a sprig from the lilac tree.

During the ride south on Greenwood Avenue, James turned toward me, and asked, "You still want to leave Oklahoma, Olivia?"

I nodded. "I can't stand the thought of staying here another second."

"If we leave, we'll lose the land we bought and paid for. The houses and buildings may be gone but there's value in the real estate."

"I don't care. The White's will steal it from us anyway. If they want it so bad, then let them have it."

We rode on in silence, until James asked, "You do know the one bright note that's come out of all this tragedy?" I shook my head, wondering how my husband could find a ray of sunshine in what I perceived to be a horrible murderous crime perpetrated against people of color, but I kept my mouth shut and let him continue. "Diamond Dick Roland? The fellow who supposedly attacked a white woman? He's free as a bird. It seems that elevator operator withdrew her assault allegation. The sheriff let him out of jail this morning."

****

Once all our worldly possessions had been loaded in a used Model-T James purchased with the gold coins liberated from the coffee can, we gathered together one last time in front of Banana John's house.

"Don't forget to send me a postcard from the Texas," Banana John said and shook hands with James.

Trying to dodge the ever-present cigar, I kissed the old man on his cheek then gave him a big hug. "We will. But if you're leaving, too, where do I send the card?"

"Care of my brother, Giuseppe Pusateri, at Ten Produce Row in the Saint Louie."

Jerome took me in his arms and gave me the biggest bear hug, ever. "Tell my niece, hello from Uncle Jerome," he said, pulling back to where I could see his sad, earnest face.

"Are you sure you won't come with us?"

He shook his head. "Thank you, but no. I'm heading north to Chicago. Maybe you haven't you heard? We're livin' in what's called the Jazz Age. I know a band in need of a horn blower. Besides, if I moved to Texas, I'd have to learn how to play the fiddle."

James shook hands with Jerome. "You take it easy, brother. Don't forget to come visit the folks."

"That's right, Jerome. When we get settled, I'll send you a postcard." Then I added, "But where do I send it?"

"Jerome Truluck, care of Joe King Oliver's Creole Jazz Band at the Lincoln Gardens, Chicago, Illinois."

"An' the Professor Swede he's-a stayin' in Tulsa?" Banana John asked.

"That's right, he'll be..." My voice trailed off. I couldn't complete the sentence. I pulled one of Mama's old handkerchiefs from my jacket pocket, wiped my eyes and blew my nose.

James filled in the missing blanks. "Professor Swede is staying here to help Buck C. Franklin."

"Who's that?" Banana John asked.

"B. C. Franklin is a Negro attorney. He's set up a law office in a tent on Greenwood Avenue. The white developers are already descending on the Greenwood District, like hungry vultures. They'll be trying to steal land from any Negro who survived the massacre."

I had finally regained my composure. "All of B. C.'s work is pro bono."

"That's-a right," Banana John chuckled. "It's-a for free."

****

Once James and I were on the road heading south into the great unknown, he looked over at me and gave me a crooked smiled. "So, you've been hoarding gold in a coffee can all this time, have you?"

I reached over to pat my husband's shoulder. "I learned that from Mama. You better be glad I'm such a thrifty wife?"

"That gold will give us a leg-up when we get to Austin."

"Austin, Texas," I said, checking out the boring scenery. "I wonder what kind of place it is?"

"Like any other, Negros on one side of town, whites on the other."

"That's too bad. We'll just have to deal with whatever comes our way." I scooted closer to James. "When we get to Austin, why don't we open another grocery store?"

"Is that what you want to do?"

"We'll call it Rose's Green Grocery. If nothing else, we'll feed the world."

Thoughts upon leaving Oklahoma

The Model T had just crossed over the Arbuckle Mountains when I glanced in the backseat to make sure my little lilac sprig was safe and secure. I planned to plant the roots in Texas soil, and hope to God it would grow. After the terrifying events in the Greenwood District, I suppose I should have been overwhelmed with sharp pangs of bitterness, including hatred for all white people. All I felt was a numbness in my heart for those who had lost everything, including the poor souls who lost their lives. I fervently hoped the racial divide that had existed would one day be healed. But deep inside, I knew the bigotry and prejudice would continue to grow unabated, until it exploded again. I settled back in my seat to admire my handsome husband, who could drive a car one-handed with more dexterity than I could with two. In all the confusion, I somehow forgot to tell James I had a surprise for him. It seems in about eight months there'd be another little Bingham in our family.

The End